JEFF P. JONES DISCOVERS T
Stories in wildly various lc
subjects are mysterious a
there are no missteps in t... ... ...

—Ron Hansen, author of *The Assassination of Jesse James by the Coward Robert Ford* and *Hitler's Niece*

YOU WANT IT DARKER? JEFF P. JONES CARRIES ON IN THE TRAJECTORY that runs from Kafka through Philip K. Dick to Cormac McCarthy (with a sprinkling of John Barth thrown in). Whether inviting the reader to comb through the dank stacks of a Stalin archive, or sweat inside the soldered-closed cab of a post-apocalyptic dump truck, or become an atom splitting from the inside, or a single brain dispersing into the universe—these brilliantly researched and deeply imagined stories are never the expected. A stunning collection.

—Janet Burroway, author of *Writing Fiction: A Guide to Narrative Craft (ninth edition)*

LYRICALLY WRITTEN AND POIGNANTLY DETAILED, *Bloodshot Stories* immerses us in the world of fable, fairy tale, and the grotesque. The characters in this wildly imaginative collection are driven by an urgency toward fates they can neither escape nor resist. In the tradition of the masters, from Poe to Conan Doyle to Neil Gaiman, Jones's ability to marry the strange to the familiar, horror to the mundane, results in fantastic narratives that defy chronology and plant us firmly in a state of wonder.

—Kim Barnes, author of *In the Kingdom of Men*

THE BOUNDARIES BETWEEN THE LIVING AND THE DEAD ARE dissolved, and resolved. Jeff Jones writes with passion and wonderful intelligence about the many characters who move through his wintery landscapes, wrestling with the human condition. *Bloodshot* is a brilliant collection.

—Margot Livesey, author of *Mercury* and *The Flight of Gemma Hardy*

SUNSHOT BOOK AWARD

FICTION · 2017

FIRST PLACE ◆ SHORT STORY COLLECTION

Bloodshot
Stories

FIRST PLACE • SUNSHOT BOOK AWARD • 2017

Bloodshot Stories

A SHORT STORY COLLECTION

JEFF P. JONES

SUNSHOT PRESS

Bloodshot Stories
© 2017 Jeff P. Jones

Published 2018 by Sunshot Press, an imprint of *New Millennium Writings*.

EDITOR-IN-CHIEF
Alexis Williams Carr

ASSOCIATE PUBLISHER | COVER & BOOK DESIGN
Brent Carr

CONSULTING EDITOR EMERITUS
Don Williams

CONTRIBUTING EDITORS AND SUPPORT
*Laura Still, Rebecca Moody, Linda Parsons,
Chloe Hanson, Joseph Mooradian, and others*

COVER ART
Harvest *by Martin Wittfooth*
68" x 54", Oil on canvas, 2012
martinwittfooth.com

   3   5   7   9 10   8   6   4   2
ISBN: 978-1-944977-23-8 (Paperback)
ISBN: 978-1-944977-10-8 (Hardcover)
ISBN: 978-1-944977-36-8 (Ebook)

www.sunshots.org
www.musepaper.org
www.newmillenniumwritings.org

SUNSHOT **S** PRESS

musepaper.org

New Millennium
WRITINGS

For Jane

CONTENTS

AS YOU ARE NOW
(SO ONCE WAS I)

He came from somewhere east of the mountain, out where strange things hide in the shadows of the hills.

Chimneys and concrete slabs, tilting barns, rusting tractors, sagging loops of barbed wire. And the dirt roads yellow in the day, pale in the night.

The snows came and covered everything then kept coming. He found an abandoned farm with a smokehouse, its cinderblocks collapsed on one side. He sat on the floor against the back wall. The only thing he felt was a deep ache, and he sat with the ache and watched the doorway. The smokehouse was very small and coated with dust, and he saw no one.

This was where he took in the world, its shapes and patterns, the waves of light and shadow passing over the place. When it snowed, the flakes flew past in a white blur—but he felt separate from it all. At night he stood in the doorway and looked out.

The white went on and on, rolled up the nearby hills and over those in the distance. Nothing moved except, on clear nights, the moon streaking across the sky.

One night something swooped in and perched on the lip of an oil drum in the corner. Its eye cavities held black moons ringed with gold. It scanned the floors then swiveled its head in his direction. When it blinked, something quickened inside him. He raised an arm.

The creature cried *Schu hu hu hu*, then lifted its wings and flew off.

When snow piled up in the doorway he rested his head on it, and when he sat up there was an outline of his ear. Best of all, when he pushed his hands into a drift, each finger left an impression, proof that he could still affect things.

❖ ❖ ❖

He walked out across the white fields, stopping every so often to look back at the stoven shafts pooled with purple shadow.

He walked a long way, crossing ridgelines and stumbling through drifts and clouting through ditches crusted with ice. He stepped on brown tangles of grass, and where the wind had scoured away the snow he stepped on bare earth. He moved as a leaf might be blown.

In a wooded draw he passed a trailer and, peering in at the windows, saw no one. An empty box, a scattering of shotgun shells, a shoe.

Around back was a shed, a blue tarp over the door-way. Inside, three house cats arched their backs and showed their teeth.

His jaws slid open, his throat widened. He grabbed for one of the cats, but it clawed his hand then streaked past, followed by the others.

He stood and looked at the shelves where the cats had been hunkered. He didn't think *cat* or *claw* or *escape*. There was a time when he would have thought in such terms, but that time was gone.

Since the smokehouse, the ache had become worse. The word *hunger* doesn't suffice. *Voracious manic craving* begins to suggest its intensity. At night when the mice nibbled on his face and arms, the ache moved through him. It tided out from his stomach in waves that reached down into his feet and up into his jaw. It pulsed in each fingertip. It was awful but somehow necessary.

Eyes closed, he would run a fingernail along the swooping line of his gums and down the long bony face of each tooth, and then he would hold his fingers in his mouth and bite them until they buckled.

❖ ❖ ❖

At night wood scratched against wood. Wind blew in the trees. Coyotes yipped. Deer stepped through snow, so fleet when startled, a leap and then gone. Occasionally, a gunshot in the distance.

And the shapes: the long thin triangle, a different shade of gray, made by the tarp edge where it pulled away from the jamb. The square at the window.

Then one night, footsteps outside, metal clanking against metal, a voice.

The words meant nothing to him—*heerkiddee kiddeekiddee*—but the voice, delicate and laced with such life, retracted his jaws. The tarp was pulled back and his eyelids rolled open.

There standing in moonlight was a small girl. Stringy black hair, little hands holding a spoon and a tin plate.

It took some time for the will, like sap in a dormant tree, to rise through him. When it did, he sat up.

...*izthatyukiddee*...

He could smell her skin, fresh, soft, and each of her organs. Inside *him*, they would quiet the ache.

Another voice came from outside, a woman, angry.

The tarp dropped back and the girl said something and the footsteps faded. The rest of the night, he stood at the window.

❖ ❖ ❖

Then one night others like him appeared. They swept aside the tarp and sniffed him and looked around at the shed. They tore the shelves off the walls, shoved cans and jars to the floor. Screws and nails spilled everywhere. They stomped glass into powder.

One of them, a female in her previous form, was bigger and stronger than the rest.

When she found a panel with a locked hasp, she took up a lug wrench and smashed the padlock until it gave. On gutter spikes inside hung shovels and hammers and other tools.

She took down a hatchet and buried its head in the neck of one of the others. It thrashed and tried to shield itself, but she kept striking until the head rolled free.

He watched all this with his hands hanging limp. Somewhere inside his dead sponge of a brain, an expired synapse quivered. It wasn't that a thought formed; it was more like a tiny light flared then died. Months later, as he touched his neck sinews, this lesson would return.

When it snowed, everything turned white.

❖ ❖ ❖

At night was when they walked, and he went with them. There were eight of them, and they traveled long distances and kept away from the roads.

When they weren't walking, they lay against each other and could feel when one of them moved, when it was time again to walk.

They came up out of the woods onto houses, trailers, barns. Many places were burned out and smelled of rot and soot. Some were still intact, though, locked and shuttered. They prowled the perimeters of these, coiling hands around doorknobs, sliding fingernails down window screens. They would pause for long moments, smelling the air.

At one house there was a dog in a chainlink run. It snarled when they opened the gate. They took from it what it refused to give.

That was his first taste of flesh. It was flush with blood and sweet, and it lessened the separation he felt from the world for a time. You could hold in your mouth and bring into yourself a piece of what you once were. The taste brought fragments flashing, in some fashion, through his senses, of soil sifting through fingers, of a lone goose honking. This was a gift. The flesh was warm and fresh, and it wasn't nothing, and you knew you must have as much as you could, that you would do anything to have more.

The putrefaction of the others now meant something new: the possibility that he could again know the wholeness that had once been so commonplace.

❖ ❖ ❖

They grew bold. They walked to the edge of town.

On a night when clouds blocked all light, they stood in reed canary grass by the creek under the crabbing black branches of a tree. Eight gray bodies with eyes and fingernails and teeth.

A silver trailer stood apart from the rest of the trailers, its windows squares of yellow floating in the dark. Only one entrance meant only one exit. They didn't think this, they knew it.

He moved with the others until his palms lay flat against the cool metal skin. Between blind slats he saw a man sitting at a table carving the skin from a potato. As he watched from outside, the ache opened into agony. He was so different from this man who had chains of blood pulling through ripe organs.

They got the door open and piled in, reaching and stumbling, moaning with the nearness of the ache's release.

By the time he entered, the man was down. He fought through and grabbed a handful and shoved it in his mouth.

In his old form, the closest comparison would've been returning home after a weeks-long pack trip of eating only freeze-dried food to a perfectly seared steak. The savor bloomed in his mouth. The veins collapsing between his teeth had only a few beats ago flowed with heart juice.

The aching subsided. What he recalled, in some manner, was how it felt to walk along the edge of a newly planted field at sunset, the purple sky red on its western edge. Soft spring earth sinking underfoot. Smells of humus and rain impaneled on the air.

Only by feeding could he again taste life's sweetness.

❖ ❖ ❖

After that they were the hunted. Men came after them and harvested two of the slow ones as they were recrossing the creek.

The remaining group stayed together and he stayed with them. They followed the strong one across fields and through woods. They traversed the hills and returned to the cat shed.

He lay on the ground, staring at the blue tarp. Lines slid along the wall during the day, and it could be said that diminished shadows, something like thoughts, slid past him as if he were the wall and the thoughts were old light moving over him. Nothing could be grasped or held, but each carried a distinct essence.

For instance, the trailer had shown him something. When the man's hot viscera touched his dead tongue—only then did he sense how far diminished he was. In his old form, he had stood in rivers up to his thighs, casting out over sun-blanketed waters, waiting for the first fish of the day to rise—and if it was a beautiful fish, heavy with flesh, he had the luxury of releasing it.

All of that was lost.

It wasn't anger or despair that accompanied such knowledge, but something less profound, a simple sense of exclusion. Somewhere something had been decided against him. The gift was no gift at all. He was caught in an arrangement to which he had never agreed—though animated by an urge fit for the living, he was lifeless.

Even now his body was passing into the mouths of other creatures, creatures who *were* linked to the life pattern but whose feeding indicted him for what he was. A clot of maggots lived in the hole in his side and would soon emerge buzzing with energy, winged and ready for flight.

At one time he had stood on his porch in morning chill and watched the dawn bleach night from the sky.

Now he was bound to this wretched compulsion, this ache already renewing. And with its return, the clarity also faded until all that remained was the need to find relief.

❖ ❖ ❖

The first thing they heard was the dogs. They took to the woods, each in a different direction.

Behind him came baying, voices, gunshots. The thick brush snagged what shreds of clothing he had left and tore them away and then it snagged his skin and tore that too, so that he wore strips of his own flesh like ribbons. He crashed through the woods like a shaggy gray stump.

He came to a gulley roofed with a mat of downed branches. As he stepped across, one broke and he plunged through. His foot lodged. He squatted there, quiet, listening.

Far off to the right there was a commotion. Reports, shrieking.

He stood and lunged with all his weight and tore the leg from its foot. After that he stumped along on the jutted ankle bone. In this way he kept going. When he found a game trail he followed it, and sometime later it started to rain.

❖ ❖ ❖

It was late that night when he came across the two. He had dragged himself a long way. The stench of a wet fire and then the flickering light drew him on. Scents of wet hair, dried meat, the warm rush of blood through chambered organs.

It was the girl from the cat shed: he recognized her smell and, mixed with it, those of dried blood and fear.

She was sitting beside a small fire holding out her hands, which were bound with rope. Her face was streaked with dirt and blood.

Across from her was a man with a rifle on his knees. He was chewing on a salted piece of meat. He smelled of gun oil and sweat.

He waited until the man was asleep, on his side with his arms around the girl.

As he crept up on them on his knees, her eyes gaped in their sockets. They were liquid and wide and gave back the glow of the dying embers like two red moons. He watched her watch him, saw his own tattered reflection in the centers of her eyes. He could hear her heart's mad suck and flush and he could smell the urine pouring out of her.

He leaned over and sank his teeth into the man's carotid artery. Sumptuous life exploded in his mouth. He pulled with everything and went in again and again until the cries stopped.

The pure, rich, glorious feast was all his, and he sated himself and beyond. At some point the girl made a sound. She was gaping at him and trembling. She said something then ran off.

❖ ❖ ❖

Far up the mountain in a brushy creek bank he found the shell of a car. This was weeks later. The car was dissolving into the earth, but he could lie across the springs in the back seat, the ankle bone planted like a cane in the floorboard, and watch the light shift and listen to the forest sounds and let the smells come.

Sometimes wood smoke, even combusted gasoline, but most often damp earth and decaying pine needles, odors that registered only as background information. The sun would warm the air and fill it with scents—squirrel fur, feather dust, antler flakings—that stirred the ache, but he no longer had the strength to hunt.

The days passed and the seasons too, and he slipped away in the mouth parts of larvae and insects. This was when he felt the contours of his neck, the gaps in the flesh, the dry slide of tendons, and he sensed the possibility of an ending. In the winter a crow came and took his eyes and he had to rely on what bits of skin were left to feel the snowflakes when they drifted in.

❖ ❖ ❖

He still had no words for the world, but a certain sense of anticipation accompanied the appearance of visitors. The scurry of feet or talons, a beak's pinch, all of it incited a reaction not unlike surprise.

Coyotes came. A porcupine. A moose pushed its enormous wet snout against his ribs. A pack of raccoons visited in the night and took his ears, and that was something new. And if they dispersed him enough, these creatures, there would be nothing left and these feelings *would* have an ending.

❖ ❖ ❖

Winter came. Snowmelt ran through what was left of him during the day and at night his bones were fringed with ice. His face was gone. His skull wore a beard of frost. A skunk littered in his chest cavity and the pups took their first steps along his spine, one vertebra at a time.

The light moved over him in patches.

Constellations he could have named in his previous form appeared in the window holes and chased each other until they dropped below the trees.

The woods and its creatures continued to move around his remains. A nearby fern leaf nodded in response to a water drop falling from its tip. A mosquito's drone cut the air. A chickadee chirped.

In the end there was no precise moment at which this strange creature ceased to exist. All the same, there came a day when what he had been no longer was, and all that came after went on without him.

❖

RIVEN

It starts in the atom, which is both oneness and manyness, where a massive bullet in the form of a neutron kicks things off by crashing through the atom's electric shields and zooming into its inner void at the heart of which, one-ten-thousandth the size of the atom itself, hunkers the good stuff, the pure matter, the protons and neutrons, quarks and antiquarks, baryons, mesons, and hadrons—all bound together by the strongest glue in the universe, the nuclear force. When the neutron bullet T-bones this core, a veil parts. Energy shakes off the material state in which it has been locked for billions of years and winks open in a new form: as the light that fuels the stars.

If split singly, the atom would have all the bluster to make a grain of salt jump. But it isn't split singly. The wounded atom, like a man hell-bent on taking others with him, fires off two of its own neutron-bullets—neighbor-wreckers, double-yellow crossers, deal breakers—that light a self-perpetuating

geometric progression. And there are so goddamn
many neighbors, trillions upon trillions, all tucked
away inside layers of banded titanium and electronics,
wrapped in a skin of egg-white aluminum and lying,
for a millionth of a second longer, under heaps of
bananas (yes, bananas, which emit a thin cloak of
radioactivity) inside a forty-foot corrugated steel
container on the deck of the *Estes*, a box-boat docked
at Terminal 46 on Elliott Bay.

What you see is a flash of light the brightness of
twenty suns. What you feel is something you've never
felt, the weight of light on your face. What you wonder,
as the ground trembles and your retinas sear, is why
there's no sound. And when the air blast couples into
you with a doomsday roar, you forget where you're
headed and what you're doing. This emerald fireball
strips you clean as it belches three white smoke rings
and rises like it was fired from a cannon inside the
earth, surging into the troposphere on a pillar of purple and orange flame. Matter locked away for billions
of years celebrates its release. Things then slow. The
fireball settles in the sky, but as its middle begins to
give off an amber glow, from out of its top blossoms a
seething kudzu of brown and gray, a great tree of dust
that expands its reach for half a mile. As the enormous
tree grows, from its branches drop chunks of buildings
and bridges, macadam and concrete, twisted bits of
steel and iron, ship containers and cranes, whole rail-
road cars and semi trucks—like so much overripe fruit.

The atom is a fantastic realm inside of which space
and time alter. To shatter this citadel is to ignite

nature's fiercest fire, so primal that it burns without
oxygen and incinerates matter—the titanium casing,
bananas, container, and ship deck—with a Shivaistic
heat, transforming all of it into a gaseous fireball.
This megaton star vaporizes everything it touches:
three box-boats, a half-dozen tugboats, two thousand containers, a crater-sized quantity of salt water,
acres of piling-supported concrete, four container
cranes, the roadways from Safeco Field to South
Jackson, and all the shops, fast food joints, and piers
along the seawall for a quarter mile in both directions. From the seagull's perspective it looks as if
Poseidon's sea-monster, finding no Andromeda as
sacrifice, took a bite out of Seattle's shorefront, its
incisors bifurcating the football stadium north-south
right down the middle.

Temperatures within the fireball's core exceed a
million degrees Celsius, cooling after five seconds
to forty-seven-hundred degrees, the point at which
rock melts. And it does melt, a hundred thousand
tons of it, spewed in a conical sheet and reformed into
tiny glass spheres that harden in the air and bounce
off the crater's rim like hailstones. Then there's the
overpressure. At thirty-five pounds per square inch,
lungs collapse, stomach and intestinal walls break,
eardrums burst. The immediate shock wave overpressure reaches three times that. Afterwinds top five
hundred miles per hour through what's left of downtown. Radiation delivered within a mile radius is a
fatal six hundred rems when four hundred fifty would
do the trick. The fireball itself rises at three hundred

feet per second to eleven miles high, morphing from sphere to donut on its way up and creating a vacuum at its center that within four minutes lofts radioactive particles, little seeds of death, into the stratosphere that will hang there for a season.

If it starts in the atom, where then does it end?

It ends with us, the people.

For it isn't like being in a dream, more like waking up from one. We're finally living in the moment. The here and now is Here And Now. We've become the stop-frame subjects of the cosmic photographer. Half a million of us sit up, turn our heads, and freeze as our picture is snapped. The Terminal 46 ship-to-shore crane operator, who banks sixty bucks an hour unloading cargo ships and who, three days ago, won eight thousand dollars playing craps at the Mukilteo Casino, is daydreaming. From the cabin suspended by a trolley over the *Estes*, he peers a hundred and fifteen feet below at where the spreader latches have over-shot the container's twistlocks because he's allowed his mind to wander to that eight grand and how he might finally take his wife to Hawaii or maybe buy his girlfriend a diamond necklace and blow it all on a wild weekend in Vegas—he's already got her bent over the dresser in the hotel room, her wrists cinched—when a blinding whiteness is the last thing he knows before vaporization. Technically he's the first to go. But who's counting microseconds?

The radiant flash, the atom's first deed, is also its quickest. At Second and University, a bike messenger, having just run her third red light of the day, is stopped mid-pedal, her tires fused to the pavement as her flesh goes charcoal. Through the twenty-first-story window of a Belltown condo, the radiant energy flashes at the speed of light so that the man balancing his checkbook at the kitchen table watches his pink hands leap into detail before they sprout a pox of blisters. At Sayres Park, five miles away, a girl celebrating her *quinceañera* has gathered her court for a photo over Lake Washington: seven *chambelanes* dressed in black tuxedos and seven *damas* wearing peacock-blue strapless satin gowns. The quince girl wears cotton candy-colored organza over a taffeta gown with a halter neck and fitted deep v-back. Their clothes determine their fate: the tuxedos absorb the pulse of light and conduct it to the *chambelanes'* skin, while the lighter gowns repulse it. Half the court will succumb to third-degree burns; the other half, including the quince girl, will survive with bad sunburns. Fifteen miles away in Issaquah, the thermal radiation pulses like supercharged lightning on a deep purple bedspread that was bought on sale, igniting it and starting countdown on the nine minutes the occupants have before flames engorge their house. Under the Alaskan Way Viaduct at Virginia Street, four homeless men splayed against the curb sharing a top-of-the-morning bottle of Mad Dog 20/20 get lucky. The roadway shades them from the flash, then collapses and folds over them as a protective concrete tent.

Close behind the radiant energy comes the blast wave, a wall of air that rides the outermost edge of the explosion with all the fury of a biblical scroll unfolding. It's driven by the individual atoms, their kinetic energies pistoning outward into a million-degree Celsius shell of vaporized debris that expands at five hundred miles per second. A force-five hurricane is a breeze compared to this wind, which breaks gas lines, smashes tanker trucks, and rips lids from underground petroleum reservoirs. The air in its wake fills with ullage vapors that burst into flame, ignited by the sparks dancing at the mouths of black-snake power lines gnashing in the city streets.

Against the blast wave, telephone and power poles, cell phone towers and traffic lights, sheds and patios, fences and trees surrender. A woman in Macy's is one step past a display window when it shatters. She drops to the floor, finds the fetal position, her cheek resting against the cool tiles, and whispers over and over, "You're okay," as if she'd sensed all along disaster's creeping shadow. On Pine a group of high school exchange students from Taipei, admiring a wax figure of Arnold Schwarzenegger as the Terminator, half his face torn away to reveal his titanium endoskeleton and red-glowing eye, are simply picked up and blown down the street like so many leaves. On Pier 69 there's a mixed group admiring the view over the water, each one of whom at that moment would agree with Sinatra that the bluest skies you'll ever see are in Seattle. There are three Germans, a Korean couple, two Russian men, a pair of retired couples from Colorado and Michigan who've known each other fifty years, a law firm headhunter showcasing the city to a software engineer from India, and two high school kids in love. One of the Russians, looking toward the hazy blue horizon that is Bremerton, says, "I like to try to memorize views like this for when I'm in places that aren't so beautiful." His friend nods and touches a hand to his eyes. The blast wave tosses them all three hundred feet through the air and unconscious into Puget Sound. In a few hours, the woman from Michigan, eyeless and naked, will bump against the side of a yacht in Magnolia harbor and be pulled aboard, the sole Pier 69 survivor.

In the King County Courthouse, a scowling judge in a black robe suddenly perks up at the light detonating on the diamond pinky ring of the man she's listening to plead his case in her office. He wags his hand in the air, fingers outstretched, pinky afire, explaining how he held their Jack Russell terrier the day it was born *in this very hand* and therefore he must be given custody. But before she can consider the merits of his contention, the courthouse is whisked away like a Lincoln Log house elbowed off a table, and the divorce case that has lingered for a year and cost the couple a hundred grand in fees is closed.

East to King Street Station there's complete destruction, no-stone-atop-another sort of thing, the blast wave and its winds fracturing and felling even steel-reinforced concrete. Columbia Tower, the concrete and glass of its seventy-six stories pulverized and peeled away, stands as a stubborn skeleton for several seconds before buckling. Farther in, across I-5, where the hospitals are, only the strongest buildings remain. An eighty-eight-year-old woman in a care conference with her husband, daughter, doctor, and social worker at Swedish, feels the blast hit like the gust one day when she was twelve and walking home from school with her little brother in Nebraska. He said, "Oh, what fun!" just before they were blown sideways into a barbed wire fence, the scars from which she still carries in her back and legs as the five of them are gathered like specks of dust and spewed through the wall.

Twenty seconds after the first atom is riven, as the mushroom cloud takes its iconic shape, as its core floats like a buoyant balloon and its edges incandesce into rainbows from all the pyrolized organic matter, a quarter million people are dead or dying. From Denny Way in the north to Seattle University in the east to the West Seattle Bridge in the south, there are ninety-eight percent casualties, most not from the blast wave itself, which Seattle's six hills toss from crest to crest, but from the afterwinds that crush and topple structures as they roar into surrounding neighborhoods with eardrum-busting ferocity. They scour the place clean and toss its constituent parts into the air like ticker tape.

Inside Pike Place Market, a woman from Chicago who's in town visiting her daughter hands a flower merchant a five-dollar bill in exchange for an armful of daisies, lilacs, lilies, and baby's breath. That morning she found an envelope in the trash, on the back of which was scribbled, *When did life become such a chore?* in her daughter's handwriting. They're meeting in

an hour for lunch at Wild Ginger, and she'll gift
the flowers to her daughter then. The blue of the
lilies recalls her grandmother, who smelled like tea
and orange peel and always used to weave barefoot
in her sewing room even after going blind at ninety.
When the light pulses, the woman realizes she's
never conveyed to her daughter a sense of her grandmother's fortitude. She resolves to tell stories over
lunch of this farm woman who set her own broken
arm and wrapped it in newspaper in the middle of
winter. In the same white instant, she knows that she
must run, if ever in her life she must run it's now, but
there's nowhere to go even if she could remember
how to make her legs work.

This is the atom, seeking its end.

As it happens, the atom's final deed is its slowest:
the mushroom head decapitates and elongates into
a dirigible-shaped mothership that sets sail on the
wind, a slow float east, sprinkling tarry rain like black
fairy dust over the country, where there are others
for whom there's still time. Still time to gaze at the
field pattern of green circles and brown squares on
the canvas thirty thousand feet below. Still time for
lovers in bedrooms and motel rooms to finish their
business. Still time for a last roller coaster ride.

Over the Teton River in southern Idaho, seven
hundred sixty-two miles from the blast, a *Culex*
mosquito infected with West Nile Virus triangulates
transmissions of carbon dioxide, heat, and lactic acid,
and hones in on a fly fisherman knee-deep in the
water. He's only passing through, will be here for

all of an hour, but the smallmouth bass are biting. The mosquitoes are like a plague, though, and the one bombinating by his ear—the one that has his number—is making him hurry through a half blood knot on his Elk Hair Caddis. As she alights softer than breath on the back of his neck and stabs her proboscis into his skin, the sensilla on her antennae detect a disturbance. She withdraws, her viral saliva undelivered, and the fisherman glances up at the day moon rising over the Tetons just in time to see a patch of the dead rock twinkle. The man, bewildered, pricks the hook into his thumb.

Somewhere over the midwest, an airplane passenger looks down on a brown-roofed farmhouse at the edge of a golden wheat field. Inside one of its bedrooms, on a bedspread of cartoon lions and tigers, under posters of his favorite rock bands, a boy dips himself into the mouth of a girl, both of their hearts gone hollow with excitement. Behind them on the girl's phone, a text appears. It reads, *Holy Shit!* A minute later, another text from the same sender crops up: *Can you believe it! OMFG!!!*

Farther east in the middle of a corn field, a man has set a metal chair and he's sitting on it in his overalls, playing his fiddle in a private celebration. It's so hot that between songs he can hear the corn growing, a sound like candy being unwrapped from plastic in a darkened movie theater, and it *is* dark for him, because he went blind five years ago but still makes his way into the field each year before harvest to unwind the tunes that remind him of when his parents were still alive, and the way the old tack room smelled, leather and oil and wool, and the way it was always somehow a few degrees warmer, probably from all the blankets, and how he stole his first kiss in there from Genevra Murry, and how it happened so fast but lasted so long in memory. Though Genevra's been dead twenty years now, he plays a tune for her, then one for each person he loved, knowing all the while that this ceremony will be his last: the diagnosis came through a month ago. That night over supper he'll hear the strangest news on the radio.

On the third floor of a community college building in a city on the eastern seaboard, a pot-bellied man with glasses, the lenses of which could fry ants, stands in front of a copy machine. He's bouncing on the balls of his feet, whistling to beat all hell, happy as a butterfly, running copies of the syllabus for his macro-economics course that starts in two weeks. From the next office he hears a colleague say, "They finally did it," and for an instant, the pure incredulity in that voice blanks him and he continues to blow but no sound comes out, only a hiss of air between his lips.

The atom is reaching still, its manyness touching our manyness. It simply won't be put back in the box. Yet through a backward glance, we can access a moment when it rested in peaceable oneness, when the twenty-year-old man who placed the mechanism in its bed of bananas in another port in another country, a man whose brother was put to death with a power drill, stood listening to the never-ending rage roaring in his head. We can't know all of his thoughts, but we can see his finger poised over the arming switch, and we can surmise that he's weighing his suffering against ours.

❖

DEAR ANASTASIA

Your mother will have told you the specifics of my failing health. What you should know is that I chose my path and I continue to choose it. Where external circumstance imposes, I tip my hat and ask the news. Nastia, what I want to tell you is the thing closest to my heart—that is, the truth—about my past and your country. It's the best way I know to prepare you before I go.

I almost wrote *before the good Lord takes me.* That's something my mother, your Grandmother Praeger, would've said. Until my twenties, I found the idea that this was a deliberate world not only true but invigorating. God and country were the twin pillars upon which I rested all other beliefs. By thirty, both those pillars had crumbled. I don't want to suggest that belief in God is wrong, just that it eventually became wrong for me. Mine is an atheism born of pragmatism. Most believers look to the beginnings of things, whereas humanists of my ilk start with a vision of the end and construct backwards.

Let me approach the question of belief this way: If consciousness is a gift, then we're beholden to the gift giver, but if it's a coincidence, then it's up to us to make of it what we will. If we see our choices not as good or bad—or even right or wrong—but as a function of *utility*, then all experience can be made useful. Whenever a person repulsed me, I embraced him as an object of study so that I might grow in understanding. Whenever I landed in an undesirable situation, I imagined a looking glass mounted in a far corner and tried to picture myself as a tiny dot upon it. Only once during the most intense period—having been given what I believe was a cytokine-based drug mixed with psilocybin—did I find myself unable to detach from the body. This morning as I stood at the window, I watched a man trip open a cigarette lighter and all strength passed from my body. Your mother rushed in to see what happened, my crutches having crashed against the glass.

Here I am already growing tired. I simply want to suggest that if you will choose your situation, even one imposed from the outside, you'll maintain the possibility of control. You'll find that what matters depends entirely upon reactions within yourself—and that these reactions, for the most part, can be mastered.

❖ ❖ ❖

Yesterday I mentioned my mother and this has got me thinking about my childhood. Imagine libraries filled with books of all kinds, streets with no checkpoints, people walking around without identity cards, public universities teaching every subject under the sun, ready loans for each student. Like my mother, I draw strength from the past.

What drew her to the past was my father. She often spoke of him, telling of pranks and stories that revealed him as a man with a big heart. In the clearest memory I have of him, we're riding in his pickup through a neighborhood—this must've been in Portland in the aughts—and we turn onto a street lined with enormous trees. The air is filled with spinning brown mittens and suddenly he's pressing the gas and laughing and we're racing through this wonderful cascade. Not mittens—leaves, I now know. We were driving through falling leaves.

Not until I undertook the task of knowing myself as thoroughly as possible was I able to trace my distrust of authority to his absence. If my passing engenders the same skepticism in you, I won't regret it.

❖ ❖ ❖

Your Uncle Ronny stopped by just now. Visitors tire me more than ever, especially ones with whom pretense is required. For his part, of course, he says nothing of my health and doesn't stand on formalities, but for me the stakes are always higher when talking with a man like him.

He acted as though it were a personal visit, a family matter. Just checking in, he said, and sat on the couch with his hands clasped between his knees. His smile recalled my interrogators' smiles after they'd discovered my fears. Gone were the ice baths and mock drownings. Dogs and live flame became the order of the day. You're too young to remember a time when most Americans would've considered such abuse cruel and unusual punishment. Nowadays no punishment is deemed too cruel, and with the force of enough years such treatment is no longer unusual. In this way everything remains constitutional. The holding camps are repeatedly deemed legal by the state powers that created them, and we have a system built on a tautology: It's legal because no one in power calls it illegal.

Security can be a mask for many sins. In the months after the attacks, I read the daily news to my mother. She was dying and we had moved her bed to the front room. She slipped in and out of sleep as I read about the latest suspension of rights or the expansion of the military commissions or the newest subversion of the Supreme Court.

One day, disgusted, I tossed the paper aside and said something like, How could this happen in a country with more lawyers than dishwashers? I'd thought that she was sleeping until, without opening her eyes, she replied that it could only happen in such a country. She followed with gibbering and fragments—by then, the medicine was affecting her mind—but I caught the phrase, *Its feet made partly of iron and partly of clay*. I recognized, of course, Daniel's prophecy, and in the special connection we shared I understood instantly her point: the American empire was now collapsing. It had grown too fast and the way had been lost.

I was telling you about your Uncle Ronny's visit. You'll forgive me these digressions, I trust, but as death nears, the urge to tell you everything grows. This letter may be all you'll have of me. Let's make the best of it, shall we? Since we'll never have the chance to converse, these notes, jotted as strength allows, are a way for you to get to know me, the good with the bad, I suppose. I'm sorry the talking goes only one direction, because I sense that you'll have many retorts and questions, but if you'll look inside yourself, we can have a conversation. After all, you're an extension of me and I of you. In that bond I tell you this—never trust Ronny. He's a government counselor, one among a legion that keeps this corrupt system in place.

To formalize this record, let me say that I, Martin Anthony Praeger, of sound mind but failing body, at age forty-eight, leave this record to my daughter, Anastasia Corinne Praeger, to be opened and read before she's placed in her vocational track. She should know that I was arrested at the age of thirty-six and spent ten years in state custody, during the last year of which I lost my left leg as a result of a self-injury initiated in protest against conditions at the camp where I was held.

What else can I tell you?

❖ ❖ ❖

As the sun set this evening, the shadows stretched and darkened on the neighborhood across the highway. The whole thing seemed to take only a few seconds though it must've been at least half an hour. I can remember as a boy watching sunsets and thinking the sun would never drop below the horizon. Time appears to increase its pace because age creates filters of experience that impede direct contact with the senses. We can't help but see the present through the layers of the past—and in this we close ourselves off.

This is why childhood's touchstone moments are so critical: they offer the solace of newness. And this is why eternity is a prison. Don't mistake me, this is no argument against the existence of God; it simply could mean that our world was created by a deeply discouraged being.

Many times in life I've retold to myself the memory of driving through the flying mittens with my father. I keep other memories in a sequence close at hand. Though we won't be able to make them together, I'm sure you'll have comforting childhood memories. Store these as wards against the whirlwind.

❖ ❖ ❖

Ronny came again today. As he was sitting on the couch, you crawled over. He very naturally scooped you up and set you on his knee. You couldn't know how that felt to me—like swallowing acid. If I had held a gun, I would have shot him. I don't know why he insists on keeping tabs, but I suspect he's been put up to it.

Communication between a father and a daughter is a tricky thing. I want you to grow up a step ahead because of what I tell you, but there's the risk that you'll model yourself not on the wisdom passed along but on the mistakes that earned that wisdom. And here we've come to my greatest fear — that this letter will do more harm than good.

What I'd like is to trace for you the turns in my thinking. What comes to mind is the summer I turned twenty-two. After graduating college I backpacked around Europe, staying at hostels and camping in cemeteries. On one of the last nights of my trip, I was in Prague, wandering through Old Town. It was overrun by Americanized shops and restaurants and German tourists and it was getting late, but I decided to buy a beer. Czech beer is the most amazing in the world. And Pilsner Urquell, drunk by the draught in Plzen Town Square, is the quintessence of beer's potential (forgive a dying man his tangents).

Picture me: tattered jean shorts loose on my hips from so much walking and meals of only bread and cheese, worn sandals, wrinkled T-shirt, a sparse beard, slinking into one of the overpriced restaurants, past the bustling servers and nattily dressed patrons to the bar in back, where you can just hear me whisper to the bartender, *Jedno pivo*. He gave me a disdainful once-over but seemed to decide that the fastest way to get rid of me was to pour me a pint. At a place outside downtown I could've bought ten beers for the same price. It cost all the money I had. As a protest I carried the beer, glass and all, out onto the square (your mother still keeps this glass in the back of the cupboard). I sat on the steps at the base of the Jan Hus monument and savored each sip. On the hill across the river hovered the castle, a glowing fortress of light. Between us lay the Charles Bridge with its statues of saints and its tower from which had swung the severed heads of revolutionaries. On the square's opposite side stood the astronomical clock that had charted time since the fifteenth century. Everything was so ancient. The day before, bending to peer at a couple rowing on the Vltava, I had noticed the spaces between the bridge's slats were filled with spider webs and the corpses of the spiders that had built them. Even the insects were old.

I started feeling the pang of having to leave, a momentary nostalgia for something I hadn't yet lost. But it was late, the beer was overrunning my empty stomach, and my thoughts pushed toward something new. That's when an overwhelming sensation struck and I suddenly sensed with my whole being the magnitude of that place. It was as nowhere in America could be: centuries of civilization pressed in from every direction—monuments, castles, theaters, cathedrals, museums. The same molecules I breathed had passed through the lungs of Kafka and Goethe and Luther and Mozart and untold kings and emperors and painters and scientists!

It's not that I stopped loving America, not at all. Instead I would say that in this moment I began loving it in a different way, not as a fixed object of worship but as a work-in-progress. Somewhere in his writings during the American Revolution, Thomas Jefferson pities his future countrymen because they'll never know the revolutionary spirit, the deep connection formed between citizen and country that occurs during the messy process of foundation. As remedy he suggests instituting a system of continual revolution in which the government is abolished every nineteen years and remade by the next generation.

This was part of what I felt that night in Prague when I allowed myself to hate my country for its excesses and to love it for its potential. When I say excesses, I mean the early indications that we were on the wrong path — the political detentions, the deportations, the secret warrants, the extraordinary renditions—things that seemed as if they would pass away with time but that opened the exchange of integrity for security (or, more accurately, the semblance of security). This isn't a new story and it occurred later in my life than in many others' lives but that's because I was sheltered growing up and naïve. No, this isn't a new story, it's an old and beautiful one.

❖ ❖ ❖

There were other signs, too: the data collection center in remote Utah, the supercomputer in Tennessee. Intelligence thrives on two things, power and secrecy. And since the fiber optic filtering centers had been built not at coastal points, where the cables come ashore, but at inland junctions in the quest to track international enemy communications, the state began sifting through domestic messages. This was in the 80s and 90s. At some point it became possible to store these messages. So they did. We're talking

about yottabytes of information. Then came the
fusion centers and centralized eGuardian database,
which transformed everyday law enforcement officers
into state informers. Mind you, these changes came
about as goodhearted, commonsensical responses
to four thousand dead Americans. You can imagine
then, after the later attacks, what became of any
impetus toward protecting individual liberties. That
giant archive, that intelligence infrastructure, that
computer inside Building 5300—they all suddenly
had a purpose. The key turned in the lock and we
finally knew what it all was for. It merely became a
matter of rounding up suspects. They started with
the immigrants, then their interest turned inward,
as it always does.

You may as well know that the charge on which
they arrested me is accurate. I wasn't in the numbers of
innocents who were swept up. I joined the opposition
after the attacks. We wanted to send a message that
the American spirit wouldn't be cowed by fear, either
of outsiders or of its own government. The legal battle
was lingering and we were losing. We cursed ourselves
for not resisting sooner. We believed that some real
strike had to be made in favor of liberty against
security. We knew it was risky and in the end we
were discovered long before our plan could be enacted.
Your Uncle Ronny tried to convince me to turn state's
evidence but I refused. It didn't matter. They got the
information they wanted through interrogation, and
they falsely claimed to the outside world that I *had*
informed on my fellow collaborators. To his credit,

Ronny continued to lobby on my behalf and procured a reduced sentence. I spent a decade of burning hell in the camps, during which time my health was ruined. We didn't know just how far until after I was released and you were conceived.

I was watching you just now as you breastfed. When you took the nipple, you fixed me with those big eyes, the color and clarity of blue champagne, so startling in a baby. I would've loved for the three of us to have moved to the country and discovered a life close to the land, but this is what we have. And living in the city is better for your mother because she's closer to her family. I can hear her in the other room chatting with your Aunt Letty. She's talking about her trip to the bazaar yesterday and how she traded some ration cards for a new outfit for you.

❖ ❖ ❖

This morning you were crawling across the floor and discovered the bookshelf. It was an enormous pleasure to watch your fingers touch some of my favorites: Solzhenitsyn, Miłosz, Soyinka. And though I'm eager to jumpstart your education, even I would admit those are heady reading for a yearling.

I can look at you and see that you're just a tiny being of flesh and slobber cooing and crying according to natural needs. Your world has a radius of five feet. What could be more self-possessed than a baby? You're insensible to the lives around you. You cry because you're hungry. You smile because something in your biology instructs you. I recognize these tricks of nature and yet I'd give everything to protect this seed of you. I would've thought that at least a kernel of common sense could be maintained, but fatherhood is the fiercest thing I've ever known. Perhaps this is how the most brutal man can be the most gentle father, encasing his children in a bubble of innocence, thinking thereby to cheat the universe out of some portion of suffering.

❖ ❖ ❖

I haven't told you about the crumbling of that second pillar. This happened before my involvement with the opposition. After the trip through Europe, I began my theological studies at a private college in California. This was a couple of years before the coastal attacks. I started by studying the theology of war, but it was the story of Job that came to trouble me the most, with its portrait of God and Satan as wanton boys and Job the fly with which they sported.

Were we granted consciousness only to find ourselves the subjects of a whimsical creator? It's in my nature to mistrust authority. I have no truck with faith. My sympathies are with doubt and dissent. Look at Job's response to having lost everything. He doesn't accept his fate (nor, admittedly, does he relinquish his beliefs). What he does is resist it by protesting to anyone who'll listen—God, family, friends. And to my mind, the only being in that book of the Bible who escapes with integrity is Job himself.

❖ ❖ ❖

I must get my thoughts down and soon. Ronny stopped by again and insisted on taking me into the neighborhood, so I piled into my chair and we went to the park. He was more friendly than usual, apologizing and fawning over every little thing. When we came across a bench, he sat. The newly sprouted maple leaves shimmered green and gray. Shadows pestered his face. I thought of the camps, their rows of cinderblock cells with thin windows. Our conversation went something like this.

"You can still help," he said.

My scalp prickled.

He said that it was better if I didn't speak, then he claimed that he had been a member of the opposition for years and that his sister—your mother—doesn't know. He reminded me that he'd procured a reduction in my sentence and claimed that he had been working on the opposition's behalf even then.

"For that I'm grateful," I said, and tried to convey some irony by gesturing toward my leg stump.

"Please," he said, holding up his hand. "You may implicate yourself."

I hate to spend precious time recounting this conversation, but it's something, Nastia, you need to know, because what Ronny revealed has repercussions for the future—that place only you will inhabit. Your mother and I met after I had already joined the opposition. I won't go into further detail because this letter could fall into the wrong hands, but suffice it to say that she's been the pillar of my life ever since. That alone puts her under suspicion.

Ronny said that he would be disappearing with Letty and their children. I watched his face for flickers of deception. His mouth turned up at the corners so that he seemed to be grinning. If what he were saying didn't carry such dire consequences for everyone I love, I would've laughed in his face. Instead I asked what he wanted. He claimed that his secret identity had been compromised and that he needed to go into hiding. One of my old contacts could help, he thought. He asked for this contact's information.

"The last thing they'll ask," Ronny said.

"They'll ask or we'll ask?" I said.

"We'll ask, of course. The last thing we'll ask."

It went unspoken that my help would constitute abetting an enemy. My instincts flickered between trust and distrust. I thought of Ronny's three children, Ellie only a month older than you. I watched his eyes to see whether they would drift over my damaged body. I decided that if his gaze broke from mine, it was a setup. Then I understood the source of his sudden sincerity: the state must be threatening his family, using him to extract a last bit of information from me. We stared at each other for a long time.

If I'm right, then the course is clear: he must be reported. Failure to do so could bring new charges against me—and this when I have at most a few months left with you and your mother. It could be that they're trying to get at her. If we're both arrested, you'll go into state custody, something I can't bear to imagine.

❖ ❖ ❖

I've been unable to sleep, thinking about the late-night visit, the men in black, the windowless van, the initial questioning and the years that follow, the interrogators invisible yet everywhere, in every waking thought and dream, in suspicions and hopes and fears. They inhabited me so completely that even when I resisted it felt like part of their plan. These days I wouldn't last long in custody. Even if Ronny's telling the truth, when he goes into hiding, the shadow he casts will engulf us all.

❖ ❖ ❖

If the worst happens and you're taken into state custody, you should know that in their sites, you're reduced to such deprivation that forgetfulness of who you are comes quickly. Expect this. Embrace it. But bury a tiny core of yourself deep inside, so deep that you forget it's there. When the time comes, it will resurface.

Here are some specifics: balance your instincts with logic, favoring logic; know your adversaries as thoroughly as possible; and decide in advance the order in which you're willing to sacrifice things. Do what you must to survive. Denounce me and denounce your mother as well. Even guilt can be put to greater use if you'll examine it as a separate entity. Imagine the guilt—or shame or repulsion—inside you as water held inside a leather flask. Picture in your mind piercing the flask with a sharp point and see the water pouring out in a stream. Feel the unpleasantness drain away.

❖ ❖ ❖

I just watched you playing with a new toy. One of the spinners kept getting stuck and you couldn't stand for that one not to rotate along with the others. You kept tapping and tugging at it, trying everything you knew to get it to spin. *Yah yah yah,* you said when I leaned over and spun it for you. Then you slapped the table with both palms.

If only I could spend these last days with you out from under this everlasting fog.

❖ ❖ ❖

What will you think of me?

The truth is, Ronny always struck me as dangerous. We met at the park today. I held you in my arms as your mother wheeled me there. She kissed her brother then strolled with you to look at the retention pond. He turned that grin on me and I told him that I couldn't help.

His face hardened. He claimed that people were starting to talk about his pending disappearance, that only my contact could give him the time he needed.

What I pictured (forgive me) was your tiny balled fists and the way you swivel your head back and forth when I call your name.

He asked whether I'd thought of his predicament, his family. Then his temper flared. He glanced at where my leg ought to be. He harrumphed and said, "I don't mean to be ugly, but weigh what you have left with what's left for me. I can take care of my sister and niece when you're gone. It'll be too late to reconsider once I'm arrested." He regained control quickly, but it was clear that he's a man used to getting his way.

When face-to-face with him it wasn't easy, but on the way back home, watching your lower lip pout the way it does when you sleep, there was no question that I had made the right choice. When we reached the house, I placed the call.

Will you forgive me for putting you above Ronny?

❖ ❖ ❖

Pounding on the door woke us before dawn. I'm ashamed to admit that the first thing I did when your mother left to answer it was to pour a handful of sleeping pills into my palm. It had been my plan all along, I realized, one I hadn't even admitted to myself. But it was Letty. It took some time to crutch my way into the living room.

She was a wreck. Your cousins were sobbing. They'd taken Ronny only an hour before, explaining nothing. As he was hustled out the door, he told her that I would know what to do—a last stab at me, I suppose.

❖ ❖ ❖

It's been five days and no word of Ronny. The irony isn't lost on me: I've bartered Ronny's liberty for your security—and perhaps it's only a semblance of security after all. In this way, I've finally been defeated. And by fatherhood of all things. The state will always win because it isn't weakened by love.

All the same, I wouldn't change what I did. I hold in my hands an official letter congratulating me on my act. It may be of use to you at some point. Please know that if it had been a matter of offering only myself, I would've done so.

❖ ❖ ❖

Under the lukewarm release of morphine, I've taken up reading about Norse mythology and the Valkyries, wild women who served Odin by flying over battle-fields on winged horses and culling their victims from the sky. There was a Valkyrie named Brynhild who was ordered to take the life of her brother. When she refused, Odin banished her to a remote hillside and there she lived her days encircled by fire. Brynhild and Job, dissenters both. If there's any deliberate shape to the world, it's of the kind imposed on it by our acts of resistance.

I had meant to conclude by spurring you toward a consideration of where you come from, but that's the petty yearnings of a father foisting empty respon-sibilities on his child. I'm watching you now as you pull yourself up, one hand on the bookshelf, the other bobbing at your side. It's your new trick, one that has made your mother and me very proud. You stand there in your little gray shorts, tottering, unsure whether to take a step forward or collapse back onto your seat. I suppose you'll do as you do.

❖

AMONG THE DEAD

*To choose one's victim, to prepare one's plans
minutely, to slake an implacable vengeance,
and then to go to bed—there is nothing
sweeter in the world. chore to because of it.*

JOSEPH STALIN

In the summer of 1999, I had the idea to investigate
and write a retrospective on the young Stalin[1] using
the recently opened secret archives as my primary
source. Though the archives are officially open, in
true Russian red-tape fashion (please excuse the pun),
access to them is extremely limited. I had, however,
the good fortune of knowing rather closely, through
past work, an historian and colleague at the Institute
of Historical-Archival Studies. Through him and

---

[1]   A number of serial killers attest to strange voices, the appearance
of evil doubles, uncontrollable sexual feelings, or deep sensations from
within their minds that begin at a young age. It is these same voices
and feelings around which the killer may develop childhood rituals
that later lead to the inclusion of victims and further acts of murder
and mutilation aimed at covering up his crimes. The more violent the
crime, the more the feelings of violence escalate until the crimes are
not enough to mask the sense of revulsion the killer feels for himself.
The serial killer lives in a solitary universe, unable to feel remorse or
empathy for his victims. From *Serial Killers: The Growing Menace,* Joel
Norris, NY: Doubleday, 1988.

my own criminological work, which is somewhat well-known in Russia (my most successful work, *The Killer Inside*, reached almost best-seller status in its Russian translation), I recently acquired a three-week foreign researcher's pass to the President's Archive. This collection contains seventy years of the most sensitive Communist Party documents as well as Stalin's personal archive and is the same one that was established under Gorbachev and later led to Yeltsin's discovery of the secret agreements between Stalin and Hitler in 1939.

To reach this most holy of holies, I traveled through the Kremlin's Spassky Gate, past the largest cannon in the world (the Tsar's Cannon, which proved incapable of firing), past the largest bell in the world (the Tsar's Bell, which cracked immediately after it was cast and never rang), and into the area that was Stalin's personal quarters. The President's Archive is kept in the former leader's apartment, a low-ceilinged but spacious complex of rooms. The papers are stored in the study, a room of pale green carpet and dark mirrors. Stalin's mottled rosewood desk dominates and bears on its worn lacquer the faint imprint of his signature—the single flourish that sent millions to their deaths—etched time and again on thin leaves of carbon paper.

The former leader keeps a stubborn vigil. I could smell his tobacco-heavy breath seeping from the walls, could feel his watchful eye on the documents I handled, could almost glimpse his olive-skinned image brooding in the smoky mirrors. Even the sheen on the desks at which I worked seemed to be oily residue from his hands.

At times other researchers moved around me: thirty-something pale ones with the ubiquitous thick-framed Russian eyeglasses; older ones speaking in suppressed tones of German, French, and Russian; and the Party ancients. These were more like specters than men. Where no one had been a moment before, suddenly one would appear, passing his skeleton eyes over a document or letter and nodding in what I could only believe was feigned remembrance. But feigned for whom? It seemed that these ancients merely haunted the research chambers in their leisure hours before death and would soon take whatever new revelations they gained with them to the grave.

My specialty is criminal psychology, and a year ago I came across this sentence: *Isolation is the stony soil in which monstrosity takes root.* The statement took hold of my mind, and several insomnious nights of reflection gave me the idea that it would be enlightening to compare the psychology of a mass murderer like Stalin with that of a serial killer. After all, if a common clinical profile could be established for these particularly disturbing phenomena that plagued our past century, future research might help diminish the looming threats they pose to humanity.[2]

---

[2]   In their study, Hershman and Lieb see a distinct correlation between the grandiose manic depression of Napoleon, Hitler, and Stalin and the manic depression of four contemporary mass killers: David Koresh, Jeffrey Dahmer, Jim Jones, and Colin Ferguson. Decrying the dominance of psychoanalysis over psychiatry in modern

It's difficult to find trustworthy information about the personal life of Stalin, this man who's had more biographies published about him than any other person, most of it Communist Party treacle. The archives contain almost nothing worthwhile concerning Stalin's youth. Three weeks of fruitless research presented me with the prospect of writing either a very shaky profile of the young Stalin or a bitter diatribe aimed at the Communist Party's proclivity for erasing its past. Frustrated, I did what all good researchers do. I took a cigarette break.

While enjoying my Marlboro in an empty doorway (as if in response to the West, Russia has also adopted a no-smoking policy in their public buildings), a gangly ancient approached. His face was long and sleek, his eyes bulbous. He wore a checkered suit.

"It seems you have an interest in Tovstukha," he said, bringing his palms together as if they were two irons placed face-to-face. They were enormous. I'm always struck by the hands of Russians. Riding public transport, I often admire the knobby and scarred hands of my fellow passengers, testaments to the hard use even city dwellers experience in that country.

Tovstukha, the man he mentioned, had been Stalin's personal secretary from the early Soviet days

---

culture and the stifling system of tenure in the medical field, the authors suggest that the overwhelming emphasis on Freud's theories in the twentieth century resulted in a lack of studies that allow us to interpret, treat, and prevent aberrant behavior, especially with respect to dangerous cases of manic depression. From *A Brotherhood of Tyrants: Manic Depression and Absolute Power*, D. Jablow Hershman and Julian Lieb, NY: Prometheus Books, 1994.

until 1935. I had turned my focus to him only the day before. Neither man had left a personal diary, memoirs, nor hardly any personal records.[3]

"I worked with him at one time," the ancient intoned, upholding the unspoken agreement of anonymity between us. "He was a gaunt, malnourished fellow. In fact we became very close for a short time before his death. He was the leader's closest confidant and all the most secret documents passed through his hands. He was a meek and studious servant in a way, but I knew him on a more personal level. He died of tuberculosis, you know."

"No, I didn't," I replied.

He tilted his head like an animal cueing on a strange sound, then laced his fingers and fixed me with his gaze as if to say, *How could you be interested in Tovstukha and not know how he died?*

---

[3] In the post-mortem phase of a crime, the serial killer is often filled with self-loathing. His violence has proved nothing and he now has a body on his hands. The serial killer often disposes of the body and evidence at a pre-planned remote burial site. After the burial, he may feel a strong need to reestablish touch with reality and will reenter his camouflaged life and assume his "mask of sanity." This mask, Norris notes, "is manifested through grandiosity or a belief in his own superhuman importance, hypervigilance or an extraordinary concern about acting morally and properly, and social adeptness to the point of extreme manipulative ability." Though the serial killer can be driven by a strong desire for acceptance, no amount of social achievement can meet his insatiable need for approval. The homophobic serial murderer John Wayne Gacy was a respected citizen known as one of the hardest working community volunteers in his town. He was active in local politics, a member of the JCs, and was grand marshal of the Polish Day Parade for several years in Chicago. During the same period, he ritualistically murdered at least thirty young boys and buried them in a muddy crawlspace beneath his house. (Norris 219-21)

"My interest is Stalin himself, his early life," I said.

The ancient's watery eyes narrowed. He brought his hands to his face and drew them along it. Then he reached behind my back and nudged me forward, muttering, "Let's go." I barely had time to crush out my cigarette underfoot. Compelled in such a manner, I had to remind myself that this was no longer the Soviet Union and that I'd not just compromised myself with an officer of the KGB.

As we made our way down that high-ceilinged, empty corridor, the shadows of forgotten men—men who not so long ago had walked this corridor with an invisible hand at their backs, their minds culling lists of recent conversations and actions—appeared at my side, their choking fear catching in my throat, their unsure hands reaching to open the high doors that revealed the inner chamber and that man sitting at his desk. His pockmarked face harbored deep pools of darkness, and the tiger-like yellow eyes reflected not another human but a corpse. In place of a friendly greeting came the words, "I hear unpleasant things, *tovarish*," and the *tovarish*—comrade—instead of a personal name, echoed in the condemned's ears like a gunshot.

I opened the doors to reveal not Stalin but two solitary researchers. We bypassed them and proceeded farther into the apartment. The ancient led us to a side room that I hadn't noticed. Inside sat a small wicker table, two chairs, and a samovar. A tiny window looked onto the blank wall of another building. The ancient closed the door, poured two glasses of tea, and we sat.

"So, you're interested in the Father…" he said and began his story:

The muddy waters of the river Kura rage past the village of Gori in central Georgia where I was born. To the north are the snow-capped Caucasus peaks, and the surrounding cliffs are heaped upon each other and worn through with dark caves. In fact, *gori* means "hill" in Georgian, and overlooking the village is a hill topped by an ancient fortress. Next to it squats a perfectly spherical boulder. It's called *Amiran's play ball* after the giant demon of destruction who inhabits the hanging mountain cliffs nearby.

I was a young boy and it was a special night in our village. My father had that day been fitted for a suit. He was a trader. Soot still lay in the creases of his shirt and breeches and in the sweat lines around his neck. In Gori, you see, tailors sprinkle soot in the street outside their shop and have their client lie in it while they sit on him. They call the impression the client's *dark twin* and take measurements from it.

My father was happy that night, but for me it held an awful foreboding. It was the first time that I recall being scared. Ever since dusk the hammers had been ringing. Outside, every blacksmith in town beat his hammer against his anvil. The ringing went on into the night, more frenzied as the darkness deepened.

"Why do they hammer so, Papa?" I asked.

"To keep Amiran from descending the cliffs," he said.

Once a year they carried out this ritual, and as a boy I didn't know such superstitions were nonsense. My mother rushed in.

"Keke's almost there," she said. She was dipping towels into the water basin in the corner. "This is her third. We can only pray this one lives."

Then, forcing its way through the hammer song burst a wild cry that sent me sprawling. My mother's face emptied.

"It's here," she said.

It was the night the baby who would be Stalin was born in the hovel next to ours. His first cries rose over the ringing of the hammers, and his father Beso, soused as usual, celebrated by screaming into the dark cliffs, challenging Amiran to descend. Beso always spoiled for a fight when he was drunk.

Later, when Soso—that's what we called Stalin as a boy—was older, Beso beat him and Keke. Beso worked off and on at the Adelkhanov Factory in Tiflis. He'd return from the factory and hear the rumors that Soso was the bastard child of one of the rich landowners for whom Keke did sewing, and Beso would give it to them both. Once when I was over there, Soso knocked over their lamp. Beso picked him up and threw him to the floor like a doll. The boy pissed blood for days.[4]

---

[4]   One theory is that the behaviors of serial killers are behaviors developed by their brains to compensate for levels of physiological and emotional damage incurred in childhood. A child deprived of sensory stimulus fails to develop boundaries between himself and the external world. While the brain is a very plastic organ, in the case of serial killers, it's unable to exert control over the primal emotions—arising from the temporal lobe, hypothalamus, and limbic region—that include fear, rage, flight, terror, panic, and sexual arousal. Damage incurred to the primal area in childhood prevents the normal development of self-control, and the serial killer sees himself without limits, all-encompassing, literally able to "walk over others." (Norris 205)

After Beso was killed in a drunken brawl, Keke beat little Soso just as mercilessly. You know, in Russian the verb *byt'*—to beat—means "to educate" as well. That became Soso's favorite word. Even after he became a famous revolutionary, he used that word in his writings.[5]

Soso's favorite pastime was *krivi*, a team boxing game. I was one of his favorites. I was big and very strong in my youth. Our gang from the upper town would box against the rich boys from the lower town. Soso hated the rich and anything to do with money. They'd always pummel us, but Soso never stopped challenging them. One time he snuck up behind one of the rich boys and cracked him over the head with a board. He nearly busted that Jew's skull open. And you know, during the Great Patriotic War when times

---

[5] In a 1915 letter to Lenin concerning the "liquidators," Stalin writes, "There is no one to beat them, devil take it. Can it be that they will go unpunished?! Make us happy by informing us that there will soon appear an organ in which they will be lashed across their mugs, good and hard, and without letup." Further, during the trials of Jewish doctors just before Stalin's death, the leader called the investigative judge and instructed him to extract confessions using this method: "Throw the doctors in chains, beat them to a pulp, and grind them into powder. Beat, beat, and, once again, beat." Both references from Robert Tucker's *Stalin as Revolutionary*, NY: W.W. Norton & Co., 1973.

Hershman and Lieb, observing Stalin's tendency for "externalization," note that by 1929, "The dictator could no longer distinguish between his ideas and the laws of nature, between his desires and the way nations develop. Reality, in effect, was no more and no less than what he said it was at any given moment as he insisted that the Communist world adopt his psychotic worldview." Such delusions culminated in Stalin's "Plan for the Transformation of Nature" that he implemented based on the false genetics of Trofim Lysenko and that set back Russian science for decades.

were very hard, I received a packet of money from the
Father with a simple note: "Please accept a small gift
from me. Yours, Soso." He was almost seventy, but
all those years and he hadn't forgotten me, his *krivi*
champion.

I'm sure you've heard the rumor that he had a
cloven hoof for a foot. Well, it has its basis in fact. Soso
bullied every one of us boys, but when anyone wanted
to go for a swim, he became very shy even though he
wasn't a bad swimmer. Why do you think this was?
I'll tell you. He had a deformed left foot. I saw it more
than once on the bank of the Kura River. I've also seen
the Medical History of J.V. Stalin that states: *Webbed
toes on left foot.*[6] It's in the next room, see for yourself.

What of his left arm? No, this wasn't a deformity.
He couldn't bend it at the elbow, it's true. That happened in Gori when he was very young. At Epiphany
one year, a great procession of mourners wound their
way up Tsarskaya Street. They were heading toward
our end of town when I realized they were carrying
Soso's limp form.

Oy! the procession murmured, Ekaterina Geladze
is cursed...never to have a son...of course, trials always
come in threes...such a sweet boy...

"What happened?" I asked one of the boys who was
tagging along beside the body.

---

[6]   Another theory indicates that psychopathic behavior may be
genetic. Research suggests that physical anomalies such as webbed
skin and connected earlobes may reflect genetic disorders of the
primal brain. "Because the development of the fetal brain takes place
at the same time that the skin develops, any skin or cartilage abnor-
malities are usually indicators that the brain, too, has not completely
developed." (Norris 239)

"Some stupid peasant let his phaeton get away over by the bridge. Nobody saw it coming. The shaft struck him in the head and the wheels ran over his arm. Boy, you should've been there, you've never heard such a sound!"[7]

I peeked through the crowd and saw that little Soso was dead. His arm was crushed and his hair matted with blood. Keke came rushing out of the house and grasped his head. She looked into his lifeless eyes and let out a wail of grief from the depths of her soul. He was her everything, you know. I don't claim to have witnessed many miracles, but that day it was a mother's love that brought that boy back to life. His eyes opened and he began crying. He recovered, but the wound turned septic since Keke had no money for a doctor. It never healed properly, and after that he couldn't extend his arm without great pain. Look closely at any photo of Stalin and you'll notice that he's cleverly masking this injury.

These are the main things I remember about the young Stalin. He was an arrogant and rude boy, but he always had a gang around him. I myself liked him

---

[7] Yet another theory posits head trauma as the root cause of aberrant behavior; in fact, a history of head injuries is one of the most strongly unifying aspects of serial killers. "Henry Lee Lucas, Bobby Joe Long, Carlton Gary, Ted Bundy, Charles Manson, Leonard Lake, and John Gacy have all had either severe head injuries, repeated head traumas, or damage that occurred during birth." Further, the neurological evidence suggests that the ritualistic patterns of serial murderers are actually mirrors of an abnormal electro-chemical process in the brain caused by head trauma. "Because the primitive brain is the most vulnerable to injuries occurring on the side of the head—because of the thinness of the skull at that point and the lack of internal fluid protection—individuals who have received sustained blows to the side of the head are often at risk." (Norris 232)

very much. The last time I saw him in Gori was at a
public hanging of two peasants. He was already attend-
ing the church school. Keke, you know, dedicated him
to become a priest, and he studied at seminary.

At this hanging there were a thousand people. It
seemed like all of Gori turned out for the spectacle.
The church school had formed their own group at the
front. The monks wanted to prove to their pupils the
inevitability of God's justice, but the ropes broke. So
they hauled the peasants back up and hung them a
second time.

I've heard that Soso became a revolutionary while
in that church school. He would have the Bible open
before him on the desk while reading the *Revolutionary's Catechism* in his lap. At night he read Darwin
and Marx by the end of a candle. He was anything
but a good student. From what I hear he spent most
of his time kneeling on pebbles as punishment. The
monks had their hands full with him, but you never
would've guessed it to hear him sing. At vespers he
had an angelic voice, high and pure. He always looked
so peaceful kneeling in the candlelight before the
golden chancel gates, singing the penitential prayers.
Yes, Soso was quite a young man.

The Party ancient had a fondness for Russian folk
songs. Before taking his leave, he gazed out the
window and sang:

> It's not spring water overflowing
> It's not a wave of the sea undulating
> It's the pagan force moving over the steppe

His voice was sepulchral and filled with the suffering of a people. It set all my nerve endings tingling:

> *And from the horses' breath*
> *The earth's moon has darkened*
> *The wind howls on the steppes*
> *The grass is bent over to the earth*

His song ended and I thanked him. We shook hands and parted.

❖ ❖ ❖

As I crossed Red Square on the way back to the hotel, the sky darkened. I tried to imagine a much older Stalin on a desperate night in November 1941, when, with German forces encircling the capital, he stood atop Lenin's Mausoleum and addressed the Red Army. I tried also to see the victory parade that, four years later, passed in review of the Father of the Nation, who was by then also the Conqueror of Fascism. My imagination failed. By the fading light I could see only spirits—hundreds of them, the ghosts of Stalin's mourners—rising like steam from the tiny spaces between the bricks into which, mad with grief, they'd trampled each other.

The largeness of the project and the smallness of my own powers overtook me. For three weeks I'd stared at letters and documents, books and telegrams, expecting to glimpse some detail of one man's youth that would act as the key to unlocking the mystery of his pathology. I'd sought incidents and stories around which a sensible psychological narrative could be built.

Part of me felt something akin to sympathy (surely not empathy) for the mistreated miscreant named Soso, who was both fiercely loved and fiercely beaten by his mother.

The most surprising document on Stalin's youth that I found was sent to me by my colleague at the Institute. It was a copy of the Tiflis Main Physical Observatory's employment record. A single entry reads, *On the engagement of Joseph Dzhugashvili, December 26, 1899.* This was a record of the twenty-one-year-old Stalin's employment as a recorder of meteorological data. As the newest employee, the New Year's Eve shift certainly fell to him. While the rest of the world celebrated humanity's entrance into the promise of the twentieth century, the young Stalin sat alone at midnight in an empty observatory, peering through a telescope into the darkness of space.

As I exited Red Square, the sky deepening to indigo, I tried to hold this image of the young Stalin in mind, to deduce his thoughts and dreams, his hopes and hatreds, a century ago. I wanted to fix him to a progressive line with antecedents and descendants; I wanted to see clearly the sequence marching him forward to his destiny. But that wasn't what resolved. Instead, that phrase continued to replay in my mind—*Isolation is the stony soil in which monstrosity takes root*—and I pictured a burst of flashes in the night sky as each person on earth, the decrepit peasant, the trader's son, the sympathetic aristocrat, the Tsar himself, was pulled into the new century. The Tiflis cannons boomed, echoes ringing like prophetic hammers, and I imagined the young man, Joseph Dzhugashvili, projecting *through* the telescope, a shadow falling among the dead and battered satellites, falling away from the living through the coldness of space and toward a black hole, its tractive power so strong that it captures all light and prevents us from ever knowing the hearts it consumes.

❖

TRIBUTE

Tilly Syreeta Bancroft
1920-2005

The first time I met Tilly, it was all about the eyes. She had the biggest, prettiest eyes in the world. They were like two flecks of sky, blue-marbled and cool. I was the third man back in the line of stunt doubles for Ray Bolger and she was a Munchkin Villager in Yellow Sun Dress. It was the morning they were shooting Dorothy's arrival at the village.

Chuck Waller, who played the Munchkinland Mayor, was strutting around the set telling people where to go and how to get there, as usual, so I opted for a quieter spot around back. On Mr. Bolger's recommendation, I'd spent the day before at the zoo's gibbon exhibit, getting a feel for the awkward grace of those lopey buggers. No better teacher than nature, Mr. Bolger liked to say. So there I was in a deserted corner of the MGM lot, hooking the back of my overalls onto a jury-rigged cruciform, when the nail snapped and sent me tumbling to the ground. Very ungibbon-like.

Fade to black and all that. Next thing I knew, there in front of me was a vision of two patches of Nebraska sky trying to resolve themselves into the most tender pair of blue eyes I'd ever seen.

"Are you okay, Mr. Scarecrow?"

The voice was as delicate as a piece of thread. I was sure I'd died and was being escorted into the blue yonder by the holiest angel in God's heaven. Her hair brushed my forehead like a tassel of golden corn silk and whisked me back to a time when all us kids would hide from each other in green hallways of corn. Tilly would agree that I bore an uncanny resemblance to Mr. Bolger, but I never could get her to admit she'd mistaken me for the real Scarecrow.

❖ ❖ ❖

After a day of shooting, Tilly and a group of Munchkin actors often unwound at a juke joint on Ventura. I started dropping by and that's how we grew close. *Oz* intoxicated all of us. The whole cast—but especially those of us who hadn't found much work until then—sensed that we were part of something bigger. She was from Ferndale, California, and I was from Red Cloud, Nebraska, a couple of small-town kids who just connected on the idea that *anything* seemed possible. *Oz* was the biggest score either of us had made since moving to la-la land.

Sure, there were blue moments. Aleister Blackwell, who played an uncredited Munchkin, would have a second vodkatini and start stroking his furry sideburns and bemoaning storm clouds over Europe, claiming that the world had passed some point-of-no-return and lost its way. We'd humor him for a while, then Tilly and I would slip off to spend time together.

We fell in love. But her family refused to bless our marriage plans. *It's not right for two people of such different sizes to come together,* her mother wrote in a letter Tilly showed me. *You'll just end up getting hurt when he tires of the novelty.*

I told Tilly that I'd gladly chop off both my legs if it would help me win her parents' blessing. It didn't seem right that our God-given bodies should stand in the way of true love, but Tilly put a hold on the wedding plans.

Things kept at a standstill for a time until the war came and I got shipped to Europe. At the dock Tilly asked to be picked up, something I'd never before done in public. There we were, me in my sharp-pressed uniform and Tilly in a powder-blue dress that matched her eyes. People gawked but we didn't care. We pressed our foreheads together. Her skin was as cool as fine china. We stepped out of time on the dock that day. I'll never forget that embrace nor our whispered promises to be true.

We wrote every day, but in the winter of 44 her letters stopped. In June came the *Dear John.* Two days later, with the 29th Infantry, I landed at Normandy. A German land mine mangled both my legs to the knees, where they were amputated. Fate had a good chuckle at that. As I rehabbed at Walter Reed, a single thought tormented and teased me—that my injury was actually a gift, that I'd been rendered

Tilly's height so that her parents would finally accept me. Sometimes I wrote four letters a day from that hospital bed.

No replies, though.

It was a long journey back to Red Cloud, but I finally made it and got through to Tilly on the telephone. She'd married Barry Bancroft, who played a Munchkin Tin Polisher and was four inches taller than her. She was pregnant with their first child. She cried and I could tell how hard it was for her, so after that I broke off contact.

She and Barry had a happy life. I saw her one last time, at the *Oz* 60th reunion. We spotted each other across the crowded banquet hall and immediately made our way past all those people we didn't recognize anymore. She stood on my footrests and we embraced. It was like I'd had a house on my chest for fifty years. I finally took a full breath.

"It's so good to see you," she said. I simply couldn't speak. People called out to each other, champagne corks popped, ice fell into glasses, and all I could do was look into those big blue eyes and feel like I was twenty years old again, lying on my back on the MGM lot, believing that dreams really do come true. To have woken up next to Tilly each morning would've made it all worthwhile. She'll be missed.

(Bancroft died of kidney failure in Santa Barbara, CA)

❖

THE SOURCE OF
MY TROUBLES

As flies to wanton boys are we to the gods
They kill us for their sport
GLOUCESTER

The sun scorched the landfill. Inside the cab of Thom's Mark IV earthmover, its windows soldered shut, the air steamed with his sweat. Trickles of perspiration rolled down the windows. Hours ago he'd peeled away the top half of his coveralls, and now his white undershirt clung to his back like a wet towel. On his boyish face sprouted a few whiskers in a faint outline of sideburns. He took a long pull from the hydration straw and swallowed the hot water like the chore it was.

It was noon. Six hours he'd been going at it. On Tuesdays they trucked in all the unmailed store catalogs. The stacks were bound in blocks of several thousand with red plastic ties that had to be broken before burying to minimize volume. Of the nine Disposal Technicians (DTs), Thom was the fastest, his youthful reflexes reinforced by an uncanny ability to see patterns in the refuse. When the trucks queued up, they sent two to him, one to everyone else. Each load could be done a little faster, he told himself. Two more loads slid down the raised beds of the dump trucks. The blocks tumbled and crashed and flipped into the pit, and even before they'd settled, Thom's eyes affixed their pattern. Within seconds his wrist was moving the black lever controlling the front scarifier, snapping the plastic ties along the predetermined line. Tuesdays, Thom felt in control. But since the memorial service three months ago, things had changed.

Thom was scraping dirt over the loosened catalogs when a gold speckle flashed in the distance. It beelined for him: a midday visit from Jimmy Dean. Bad news. Jimmy skidded to a stop in his Eddie Bauer Special Edition golf cart pimped out in authentic gold trim, and he stepped from the cart. Black boots, tight Levi's, a crisp white button-down, and a yellow cowboy hat that shaded everything but his sharp nose, which jutted over a black handlebar moustache. To Thom he looked like a bipedal mosquito.

Arms crossed, Jimmy leaned against his cart and touched the mic at his lapel. The words crackled over Thom's cab speakers. "LRC just dumped a pile of Huggies up by 5f. You want to make a few passes, Number Six?"

Thom's face burned. That order could've easily been sent remotely; Jimmy had only driven out here

to see his reaction. Plus, *make a few passes* meant
spending the next eight hours wallowing in four
tons of baby shit. No doubt they hadn't *just* been
dumped, either, but had been cooking all morning.
The maggots would already be teeming. Lately, every
miserable assignment landed at Thom's blade.

"I got these catalogs I'm dealing with," Thom said.
"Besides, I did the last diaper load."

A smile flickered across Jimmy's face. "That wasn't
a request."

Thom tightened his grip on the gear shift ball, felt
the thrum of the fifteen-hundred-horsepower engine
in his palm. Jimmy used to brag about Thom's effi-
ciency in front of the other DTs. "Double wages if
you can beat Thom-boy here," he'd say at the morning
briefing. Thom used to get the best assignments and
even afternoons off when things were slow. Jimmy
stared up at Thom, where he hovered above ten-foot-
high tires. A single wrist flick would squash Jimmy
like a bug.

"Don't make me repeat myself. You're on diaper
duty, kid." Jimmy sped away. The pages from strewn
catalogs flopped in his cart's wake like a flock of
maimed birds. Thom imagined Jimmy speeding
back to Portable 5a, strutting in the door balls-first,
calling Agnes "Honey," and telling her to crank up
the swamp cooler a notch.

At times like that, Thom dreamt of doing terrible
things to Jimmy, things that would fill us all with
dismay were I to go into needle-nose-pliers, fingernail-
plucking detail. It was then that an image would pop

into his mind of Agnes sitting at her aluminum-panel desk, the one with the faux-woodgrain sides peeling at the corners, and he would sense a calmness. Every other Friday, when Thom stood in the paycheck line with the other DTs outside 5a, he gazed through the trailer's picture window at Agnes. If the sun's setting light managed to slip through the diesel fumes, it lit up her skin so that it glowed, bronze and rich. It was an odd thing, that vision of Agnes, but somehow it always cooled Thom's jets.

He pictured Agnes at her desk in 5a. Years of back-filling had built up the earth around the portables so that the trailers sat in bowl-like depressions off the main access road. Agnes's desk faced the thirty-foot slope that poised like a tsunami of dirt (an arrangement that will become important in just under four thousand words). Whenever Thom passed 5a, Agnes never failed to glance up and wave, and that always made Thom's heart swell.

Three months ago, Agnes's husband, who'd been a Dean, was crushed to death by an emergency vehicle during a citywide safety drill. The DTs got the day off to attend the memorial. Except for the Rev, they were all in love with Agnes. Thom fell for her four years ago when he stepped off the Labor Resupply Center (LRC) bus, having been reassigned from sewage management to solid waste. Now, as he drove across the field and demolished Jimmy's puny cart tracks with his earthmover, he could picture Agnes's eyes, such a deep indigo that they shaded into black. His ribs strained to control his thrashing heart.

At the service for Agnes's husband, Thom sat in the last row. He kept his gaze on Agnes, who was surrounded by Deans. Every few seconds she dabbed her eyes or leaned over and whispered something to her daughter Cleo.

The pasty wisp of a minister kept talking about the "valuable service" the deceased had given and the "better place" to which he was headed as a result. Thom knew Agnes's husband only as a picture on her computer screen, a man of medium height and a rugged complexion, posed with Agnes and Cleo beside an enormous smiling rodent.

After the service all the DTs filed out and loitered in the parking lot, ogling the stretch Humvee Jimmy had rented for the affair. The Rev was reclining against his old Dodge pickup, smoking an unfiltered. The Rev had worked in waste longer than anyone.

Thom ambled over and asked the Rev to what extent he thought they could ply the memorial for some further PTO. The Rev looked crosswise at Thom, because they both knew the answer, and made an observation of his own.

"The next attempt will seek not to transfer the corporate-state edifice from one hand to another but to smash it, comrade," he said.

"Is that right?"

"Small acts of local retribution are the precondition for every real people's revolution. That man in the box was a principal contributor to exploitative hierarchies." The Rev was a walking stockpile of Unpatriotic Feelings (UFs) and a genuine hazard to be around, but Thom knew him to have a good heart.

"What did you make of the minister's words?" Thom said.

"Horseshit. Our goal's a working-class government, a thoroughly flexible political form since all previous forms have been essentially repressive. The secret is this: the system we plan is the result of the struggle of the first-world working against the first-world consuming class, the political form at last discovered under which the economic emancipation of all labor will be accomplished."

"You don't say," Thom said, then wondered aloud whether such thoughts weren't ripe with Hazardous Thought (HT), Mockery of National Security Concerns (MNSC), and even some FHJ and CUD, and, if put into action, might hamper the efforts of the Minor Opposition Party (MOP), whose ultimate goal, everyone knew, was to oppose harmful government and make life better for everyone.

The Rev flicked a yellow jacket from his sleeve and glared at Thom. "You may think all I do's push other people's pig-swill around all day like most of you dipshits, but all the time I'm burying castoffs, my mind's going at the speed of light. You know what I'm studying?"

"What?"

"The squander. Next time you're burying empties, try this. Imagine yourself as an eagle soaring miles over the earth, peering down, and observing the whole human operation, the city with its precisely ordered streets, its concrete and steel boxes, its manicured lawns and walled-off warrens. Then see the lines of trucks streaming out from the city, carting load after load of castoffs. And ask yourself this: Why do I keep showing up for work, day in and day out? What're you waiting for, comrade? Don't be a reactionary. Be a revolutionary."

Something about the Rev's words made Thom's skin prickle. He never could follow such convoluted ideas, but this last point, of taking a fresh look at the waste, seemed like a good idea. Then he sensed something like a sliver of glass lodging in the back of his neck. His legs gave out. The asphalt dug into his knees and suddenly loomed inches from his face. His throat felt like someone was shoving sponges down it. A yellow fog closed over everything.

❖ ❖ ❖

Thom awoke in a hospital room with the Rev standing over him.

"Son, you need to stick around. You've got work to do yet." He told Thom about the yellow jacket that stung him, his collapse in the parking lot, and how Agnes, exiting the building, had rushed over. She dabbed Thom's head with her handkerchief and insisted on using the Humvee as a hospital transport. Jimmy was livid at having the vehicle co-opted for a lowly DT.

"That goldbricker has got to go," the Rev said.

Thom touched the place where Agnes's hanky had graced his skin, her tears mingling with his sweat. *It's true,* he thought, *her love's as real as mine.*

As he rumbled toward the diapers Thom looked toward 5a. Agnes (exiting in two thousand eight hundred words) was probably fending off Jimmy's groping at that moment. The trucks continued to stream past the front gate. The line extended onto the plain that lay between the dump and the city.

Like a flu fever, the first inkling of something close to despair settled over Thom. Fingers of diesel smoke linked the trucks, and the sun sparkled off their windshields so that the caravan looked like a row of stars stretching to the horizon. What would the world be like without him and others like him in it? If there were no DTs, no Mark IVs, no TRDs or WMSs or BHQs, what would happen? People would pile their garbage in the streets. When one city got too clogged with garbage, they'd move on. And given enough time, what would happen to all that refuse? Wind and water would return it to the soil. It might take longer, but the earth would reclaim the waste. Wouldn't it?

Thom went back to work after recovering from the yellow jacket sting. Two weeks later, Agnes returned too. On payday Thom stood in line outside 5a, holding a dozen red roses that cost him a week's salary. When it was his turn he climbed the aluminum steps and handed the flowers to Agnes.

"These are for you," he said. "I wanted to say thank you."

"They're beautiful, Thom. What a sweet boy you are."

Boy? Sure, she was four or five years older, had been married, had a daughter, and was a widow, but they were about the same age. "I hope you like them," he said.

"They're perfect." She reached across the desk and patted his hand. Her fingers felt light and soft. She rummaged through cupboards, saying, "I know there's a bottle I can use as a vase here somewhere."

Thom was about to say something else, something brilliant, when Jimmy peered around the corner. At sight of the roses, his moustache ends flared.

"Where'd you get that kind of dough, Number Six? We paying you too much?"

"I had a little saved back."

"Then maybe you should've chipped in for your little ride to the hospital. You know how much that Hummer cost?"

Thom flushed.

"Oh, Jimmy, let me have my flowers, will you," Agnes said.

Jimmy gripped Agnes's elbow, then leaned over her shoulder and stabbed his nose into the bouquet. Thom's throat contracted.

"Can't smell nothing," Jimmy said. "Sure these are real?"

"Of course they're real," Agnes said, swatting Jimmy's shoulder. "And I'm going to keep them for as long as they last."

Ever since, Jimmy had it out for him.

Before he turned off the access road, it hit: a sickly sweet all-consuming reek. Thom gasped and tried to breathe only through his mouth, but still the smell boiled through the cab vents and permeated the air.

Past an earthen mound, there they sat, a pile of Huggies as high as an office building, steaming in the
heat. A rotten stew.

He stopped the tires an inch from the white wall.
The pile expanded and shifted in the heat. The squishy
diaper innards would, under compression, splatter
over everything. By the time he finished, his beautiful
Mark IV would be covered tire-to-tailpipe in baby
shit. The windshields would be a bleary mess and
the air system would stink for days. Even with the
pressure hose, the crust would take an extra hour to
clean. Thom would miss the last bus home and have
to wait through the late shift for the next one. He
dug in his coveralls pocket for a cigarette.

Thom could afford one smoke a day. He spent
mornings planning when to take his cigarette break,
longing for that first pull, the way the smoke spread
down his throat and into his lungs.

He lit the tobacco, put the filter to his lips, and
breathed a full breath through the cigarette's burning body. Thom pictured what Wednesday would
bring, all the discards that would be hauled out
load after load: the delectables that made his mouth
water—half-gnawed chunks of Syntha-Chicken,
sticky tubs of Häagen-Dazs, syrupy Cyclone
Cakes—as well as the other more substantial throw-
aways—oxikits, homewalkers, lead-lined jumpsuits,
baby respirators, jellybags, and so much more. Even
though he could never afford such things, in his
first couple of years as a DT, he'd memorized their
descriptions from the catalogs that had lodged in the

rails of his traction bars and which he had pilfered and secretly studied.

His mind responded to the cigarette: it had some quickening power. He thought of his reassignment in six months. Maybe he'd be sent to a Waste Transfer Station (WTS), where the retrievers got to soar over piles of discards and pull out Improperly Disposed Objects (IDOs). He had heard that, hooked into guy wires, they looked more like moonwalkers, bouncing around and pulling out surveillance bracelets, reusable scraps of real wood, or relics like fishing rods. He hoped it wouldn't be to some of the awful places he'd heard about—meat factories or crematoria for strays.

Underneath him the machine rumbled. He loved his earthmover, so powerful and responsive. He knew that he should start in on the diapers. Instead, he took out a second cigarette and lit it. He pictured the discards after a million years. By then they would've melted into a layer of tar-like sludge. Maybe the descendants of humans, who would be sleek and whip-smart, would dig up the sludge and use it to do something brilliant, like fuel spaceships to the stars. Halfway through his second cigarette, the tin voice crackled over the cab speakers.

Video surveillance.

"What the hell's the problem, Number Six?"

Thom wished for the hundredth time that he could reach through those speakers and grab Jimmy's scrawny neck and squeeze until it collapsed.

"Because you can be on your ear tomorrow morning if you keep lollygagging."

The story around the yard was that Delilah and Lester Dean named their son Jimmy in the hope of impressing the old-money meat relatives, and in fact the ploy had been enough to secure a loan that kept the dump afloat during tight times. The Deans never saw a penny of the sausage money, though. They made their family fortune burying other people's garbage.

"Don't bother me, Jimmy, I'm about to have an epiphany."

"I'll give you an epiphany, numb nuts. Get back to work or you're fired. How's that?"

With his mention of "epiphany," a word he'd picked up in an advertising jingle, Thom realized with something approaching starlight clarity that either he was in control of his life or he wasn't. It was as simple as that. He just needed to make an unexpected choice to test this idea. He looked around for something he'd failed to notice before. His gaze settled on an unblemished section of the dashboard just above the lifter's hydraulic pressure gauge. He took the cigarette's cherry tip and touched it, sizzling, to the dash. It sent up a thread of black smoke.

Outside, the diapers towered. Thom pictured just driving away. A shiver passed through him. The impulse to refuse, to say no, struck with such a force of temptation that he gave in. He simply had to choose. He could choose to do *anything*.

Thom's revelation is important. Otherwise, why concern ourselves with this particular Tuesday in his life? Previous Tuesdays only demonstrated patterned monotony: shining fog-lights in pre-dawn darkness to split bundles of catalogs; scraping them with his front blade into a pit; burying and compacting; then ripping a new hole—all day long through the heat and fading light until darkness and exhaustion. Then there was the snoozy bus ride to his tiny room in the quarters on the city outskirts, a bland meal, and five hours of sleep before Wednesday morning arrived. But *this* Tuesday, as Thom flicks the cigarette butt onto the floorboard and the narrative moves into present tense in an attempt to reflect the sudden immediacy with which he's experiencing events and the nearness of the approaching climax (one thousand four hundred ninety-three words), *this* Tuesday becomes different.

As Thom makes a wide, swinging turn away from the diapers, he indulges in a fantasy. Agnes and he walk beside the ocean, each of them holding one of Cleo's hands as the waves roll up on the shore and the sand caresses their bare feet. They don't say anything because they're in love with each other and their new lives. Then Cleo spots something that has washed up in the surf, something blue and sparkly, and she breaks free and races for it. Thom follows, running after Cleo with Agnes watching, all of them stunned with joy. Foolish? Of course. But who hasn't done something foolish for love?

The speakers crackle. "Where the hell do you think you're going?"

"I need a hand," Thom says. "Can you meet me on the access road? I've got a loose belt."

"Maintenance issues go to the garage, jerk-off."

"It's a quick fix. If I take it to maintenance, I'll be down the whole day and them diapers'll never get buried."

A pause unspools like a thread between them. "You're spoiling for trouble, Number Six. This better be quick."

Thom smiles. He isn't usually so crafty, but as he approaches the access road hovering over Portable 5a, his confidence rises. He climbs out of the cab and loosens a lifter belt. Jimmy Dean switchbacks up the hill, pulling an angry tail of dust into the air behind his cart. Jimmy steps out and climbs the cab ladder. Sweat rides his forehead like a row of buttons. A scowl underscores his moustache.

"You're stretching my patience thin as paper," Jimmy says.

Thom leans into the cab, swiftly pockets the ignition key, then grabs the crowbar from behind the seat. "When I give the sign, pull the lifter bar up so I can wedge the belt on with this."

"This is going to cost you," Jimmy snarls, standing eye-to-eye with Thom. One of the sweat buttons pops free and rolls to the tip of Jimmy's nose. Then, together, they notice a cluster of dark clouds in the west. "Just great," Jimmy says and horks a wad of phlegm over his shoulder into the dirt. He climbs into the cab. "Let's get this over with before the storm hits."

Thom shuts the door behind Jimmy as fast as a cat. Then he wedges the crowbar against the frame to lock it shut. Thom leaps off the machine. Pounding and muffled shouts follow him down the hill, but the joy of running floods through him. It's real, that joy, and he can tell because his boots don't touch the ground. Gravity is no match for his love of Agnes. Then she's there at the bottom of the hill, holding open the trailer door as he floats up the aluminum steps. They stand inside and stare at each other.

"Thomas C. Ruben," she says.

Her eyes set his heart pounding so hard that he expects it to split open his chest and land, glistening, on her desk. "I've locked Jimmy up in my cab." This sounds so ridiculous that he snorts. Soon he's laughing harder than ever, buoyed on waves of hilarity.

"You did what?" Agnes walks to the door and peers uphill. The rain has begun falling in gray streaks. The bewildered look on her face pries open a hole in Thom's stomach around which the giddiness swirls before it drains away.

"Agnes, I need to ask you something." He takes a deep breath, feels the world expand. "I'm in love with you?"

A corner of her delicate mouth twitches and turns down. He watches his hopes slide into that crease and fall away. She has never loved him. Never even considered it, apparently. It makes sense; she was always just as friendly with the other DTs. "I think you'd better let Jimmy out. He's going to be hopping mad."

Thom feels like he's being scolded for not properly cleaning his work space. The rain patters on the trailer roof.

"Agnes?"

"Yes?"

"Will you remember me?"

"Sure, Thom, I remember you."

Thom reaches for her hand. It's fragile and warm. He bends to press his lips to it and feels the tug of resistance. He kisses it anyway. "I'm sorry," he says, then leaves.

The trek uphill takes forever, a plunging slog through rain-loosened dirt. Rivulets score the steep bank, little slurries of mud. By the time he reaches the access road, he can see the cords on Jimmy's neck. He's blistered with rage. Four other golf carts, carrying the managers from 5b, 5c, 5d, and 5e, climb their respective hills and spit jets of mud as they head for the access road. *Should've disabled the radio,* Thom thinks. He lifts the crowbar.

Jimmy throws open the door. "You're finished, ass-crack. You're going to be so far gone, you'll never find your way back. I hope you like grass clippings."

Everyone's heard of such assignments. Shards fill the air, stick to the skin, creep into every orifice. The stench is so bad that you get a five-year headache.

"Park this thing, then get out of my face," Jimmy says. "I don't ever want to see you again." He jumps into his cart and zigzags down the hill. Thom watches in silence.

Any future Thom might've had is wrecked. He'll go to a grass-clipping repository and breathe glass-edged filaments the rest of his short life. Or perhaps he'll be sent to an animal crematorium, where one day in his nth month, he'll throw himself into the furnace behind the carcass of a brown-haired mutt with a missing ear. A common belief among many cultures is that stories breathe their characters into existence. Only arrogance denies such power. And why not in a universe where only five percent of the matter is accounted for, the rest lurking in the ever-expanding mysterious dark energy and dark matter, why not posit worlds birthed by storytelling?

Jimmy skids to a stop and freckles the front of 5a with mud. The other managers, in customized carts of their own, sail past Thom, flash sneers and fists and middle fingers through the rain, then zoom down the hill. They pull in next to Jimmy, who leaps from his cart, beats his hat against his thigh, wipes his brow. He points up the hill and hollers threats.

Thom considers his situation. Perhaps he got off track at the diaper mound. It seems like it was earlier than that, though. Maybe the memorial service. But that was just an extension of his feelings for Agnes, which began four years ago. Maybe it was his love for her that put him on this path. Or maybe the whole thing was set in motion before he was born. Or it could've been those intoxicating beads of sunlight on the truck windshields. Could the Rev's words finally be settling in? The cigarette's magic seeping into his brain's corners?

Thom pictures again those creatures into which humans will evolve. Beautiful beings, efficient and graceful. He gazes at the cloud bank engulfing the sky and imagines them swimming there in the air between droplets of rain, unbounded by physical laws, space, distance, even time. He wants desperately to join them—and if not that, then to please them. He feels the quickening of his blood, the heat in his palms. He conceives of a final choice that might speed the coming of their race.

He climbs into the cab. Jimmy's odor, musk and axle grease, fills the air. With three quick hand movements, Thom starts the engine, bumps up the throttle, and veers off the access road. He aims his Mark IV downhill.

The machine sinks half a foot into the wet hillside, and in this he loses his advantage. He throttles up. The tires slip. Precious seconds tick away. By the time he should be there, he's only halfway. One of the managers points. He must gain ground fast. He shoves the throttle full, sends its motor into a din of stuttering combustion. Gravity finally starts to work for him, speeding the earthmover and allowing the hillside's crust to bear it up. Inside the cab Thom leans forward, his forehead pressed against the front glass. He charges brow-first like a bull down the hill.

Jimmy's eyes rim white. He dives into his cart and stomps on the gas. The cart churns mud and scoots away just as Thom swipes the air with the scarifier. Desperate and ineffectual. Six feet away, in the picture window of 5a (seventy-five words from death), stands Agnes, one palm pressed against the glass as she searches the scene. They'll never play in the surf with Cleo and plan their lives together while sand pushes up between their toes. The last glimpse of

Agnes sears onto the lens of Thom's inner eye. Ceiling bulbs halo her figure in a stream of fluorescent light. Her eyebrows raise as if she'll ask a question.

Then she is (one word) gone, along with 5a. Buried under a pile of shattered wood and bent aluminum siding. The rain gives way to downpour as hands claw Thom from the cab. His face sinks into the mud and blows land wetly against him from all sides. But no physical pain can penetrate the darkness into which he travels.

As his skull cracks under the heel of a cowboy boot, Thom decides that whatever or whoever made him is, at best, a whimsical creature acting without rhyme or reason and, at worst, a malevolent agent bringing misery not only in this life but also the next. Thom's final sensation before slipping into coma and then oblivion isn't reducible to language but something more like the purest expression of terror, a fear rising up from murky depths, the sense that he's going someplace that has no pre-established patterns, where he's in control of everything but there's nothing but himself to control. And he's going there alone.

❖

SNOWMELT ON ICE

I.

In the fall of 1925 after a long pursuit our forward detachment overtook the remainder of the white soldiers between the Iazguliemskii and Rushanskii Ranges. The exhausted band of men were holed up in a glacial cave and had agreed to surrender when suddenly a commotion came from inside and gunfire erupted. Assuming this was an attack, our units opened fire.

LETTER FROM GENERAL (RET.) M. S. TOPILSKII TO
A. G. PRONIN, DIRECTOR OF GEOGRAPHICAL STUDIES,
LENINGRAD UNIVERSITY, 1940

Ermolai waits on the glacier, letting the seasons come and go. He never believed it possible to differentiate one beat from another, but in the heart's absence he's found that nothing is ever completely lost. In time, each living beat has become distinct and, with effort, accessible. The recall starts subtly, as insignificant as bee's wings thrumming against the skin, before reviving other familiarities: the smell of decaying apples, the collapse of a berry between the teeth, the crunch of glass underfoot. Then the memory will open onto a moment in which bursts the full sensation of the heart drawing and flushing blood. It may take several days, but when he isolates a single heartbeat, he can feel the blood being pulled like a string, like many connected strings, through the channels in his body.

He's been dead for decades. Perished. Transformed. Suspended in time, which flows like a languid river, compelling him and the elements around him, in snow crystals and rock and soil and tiny plant leaves, forward in its stream. His death came by a bullet that crashed through his ribs and lodged in his gut; his life seeped out through the hole it opened in his side. He waits because the bullet should've never been fired. He wants others to know the injustice of his demise. He'll wait until they come. They will come. They must come.

❖ ❖ ❖

He stands vigil in the cold as the wind and ice whip. Once in a great while the winter touches something in him that causes a shiver. Or perhaps it only stirs the memory of a shiver.

The lack of companions would bother him if he hadn't grown so close to the glacier, the water percolating in its pores, the ancient crystals dissolving, the new layers forming. At times during a night storm when the moon rises occluded but bright, its light captures the snowflakes as if falling from the stars, and they appear not as crystals but as bodies hurtling through the sky, spinning, grasping for each other, clumping in groups, and driving, locked together in wounded spirals, into the mountain. They land like manna on its skin and dissolve briefly into *snezhnitsa*, snowmelt on ice. Wind cools the *snezhnitsa*, new layers compress, and the glacier grows.

Only a few spirits have wandered into these reaches, but none could keep him company, distracted as they were by the loss of so many things. Most of them were *zalozhynie*, outcast children who'd died before christening. If he did miss people, it would be the press of a crowd along Nevsky, the pleasant surprise of recognition at seeing a familiar face, the arching of the eyebrows, the skin wrinkling into lines around the eyes.

In the days after his death he followed the men who killed him out of the mountains, watched them huddle together at night and stand guard by the fires. Soon, though, he fell away and wandered instead among searing white cliffs, talus slopes, black-rock canyons, over slopes covered with juniper, wild roses, and hawthorn, and into villages where he watched people sip carrot tea and mend ropes. The farther he traveled from the glacier the more unbearably empty everything grew. He thought about returning to Petrograd, but what was the use? The only place that held meaning for him was the place of his transformation. In death he connected to the glacier; even many versts from its slopes he can feel its ice-locked veins freezing and unfreezing. So he waits, imagining the men who will come. They'll breach the frozen layers and vindicate his waiting.

❖ ❖ ❖

One day in the first decade as he gazed at a washed-
out sky, he found that he could relax his hold to
distinction, like allowing the mind to blur, and the
glacier's banded layers would rise up around him like
incoming tidewater. In the glacier's upper levels, thin
layers of snowpack slip against each other and liquefy
at the seams; the melt trickles through cracks and
flows deep into pitch-black channels; wide fractures
and gravity-warped planes of ice wend through its
middle in magnificent curves like sheets of paper
wind-wrapped around a tree; and to his great surprise,
in the glacier's deepest parts, there's heat, released
from the ice and rock being crushed under its own
enormous weight.

Inside the glacier, he has come across petrified trees,
frozen animal carcasses and plants, and an endless
variety of stones. Yet there are places he won't go:
the graves. He fears the sensations of knitted bone,
frozen flesh and hair, the thickness of organs, all of it
drawn downward as if converging on some white-hot
engine below the ice. He imagines gravity eventually
will lead him to the heart of what lies beneath the
glacier, but the force is eternal and it will wait.

Sunrises, like the seasons, come and go. Some
days depart without a single thought, only emotions
shifting as the wind blows tails of snow into the
air. He thought at first that time might pass faster,
but each twilight stretches out longer than the one
before. More and more he must remind himself
that he's Ermolai Vasilievich Michko, son of Vasili

Mihailovich and Iana Petrovna, and that his thoughts and memories are still things with substance.

II.

In 1957, Pronin was elected chairman of the Snowman Commission and that year led an expedition to the Vakhan Range in the Pamirs.

GREAT SOVIET ENCYCLOPEDIA,
"PRONIN, ALEKSANDR GRIGORIEVICH"

A tiny silhouette appears by Stepan's grave. Others join it, clustering atop the ridge. These are the ones he's been waiting for, the seekers.

Ermolai pictures the trail leading to that spot: a track cut into a névé slope he hiked with his fellow soldiers. Three days before they reached this slope, they had been far below on the river road. Their pursuers, with horses and oxen, had been gaining, so Colonel Sorotov ordered them off the road. They began climbing the mountain and though no one said so, they all hoped that the enemy, faced with abandoning their mounts, would give up. Instead they accelerated the chase and followed them as the path narrowed where it hugged the cliff. The fittest squadron guarded the regiment's back and fell into skirmishes in such tight places that daggers were more dangerous than rifles.

They'd eaten their last real food—dried apricot and lamb for which they'd traded cartridges at a

Wakhi village—more than a week earlier. Since then it had only been the crusty loaves stuffed in their pockets. Ermolai imagined the snow dust clinging like moss to their felt overboots would be the soil for their graves. His cousin Stepan, as a lieutenant, hiked ahead with the officers. For two days they pressed on through blizzards and white outs. When they crossed open fields, ice cracked like small trees underfoot. Men plunged into hidden crevasses. Some tied ropes between themselves. Others, terrified or exhausted, simply gave up and slumped aside in the snow. Still others entered an icefall maze of blue stalagmites, sheer faces that rose like buildings, and never emerged.

On the third day after leaving the road, scouts reported an ice cave ahead. None of them could've made it much farther. They trudged upward, and as the soldiers ahead of him attained the ridge, their shadows blurred against a white sky, creeping along in single file. Then there was a shot. One of the shadows fell. Word soon passed down to Ermolai that this was Stepan. They said that as Stepan high-stepped through powder snow, his officer's revolver misfired. The bullet struck under Stepan's chin and passed through the top of his skull. Later, after his own transformation, Ermolai understood that Stepan saw the cave and, understanding something of their fate, simply shot himself.

By the time Ermolai got to him, Stepan's face was frozen, his brows beetled, his lips pressed forward. He yanked away the grave-digger's ax and began hacking at the ice. The cold seeped through the handle into his finger bones and numbed his hands. A caul of sweat froze on his face. He cut a knee-deep grave, then rolled Stepan's frozen corpse into it. It seemed that a prayer should be said, but he couldn't muster the strength. He merely trended along the path the others had made, plodding down from the ridge and up the other slope.

Ermolai stood at the cave entrance and watched their pursuers appear one at a time on the ridge. Like ants, hundreds of the enemy swarmed over Stepan's grave. A group of twenty clumped around a *tachanka* they had somehow tugged by hand the whole route. Its spoked wheels were clogged with ice, yet they hauled it halfway up the slope, the gun's dark eye gamboling from the bumps and jolts. They waved to taunt him. He stared belligerently back while the remainder of his regiment sought sanctuary inside the cave.

❖ ❖ ❖

The seekers encamp over the remnants of the cave mouth. They move unnaturally quick, their overcoats slick like glass. Their actions seem superfluous, flighty even, and they communicate without discipline. They pound stakes into the ice and jerk open canvas shelters. They study maps and charts, peck at odd instruments. The man who appears to be the leader stands on the ledge outside the cave. His long gray beard flutters in the wind, and a V-shaped vein over his left brow pulses. His yellow wolf's eyes survey the ridge they just crossed.

In the hours before he died, Ermolai gazed upon
the same ridge, watching as the reds trampled Stepan's
grave. Summers when Ermolai was a boy, he went to
live with Stepan's family, who served as caretakers of
an estate south of Petrograd called Chernokolodez.
The owners only lived there in the fall and winter, so
the visits were a time of carefree frivolity, the best
part of each year. Though Stepan was two years older
than Ermolai, they were as close as brothers, and they
roamed the orchards and woods and skinny-dipped
in the ponds. They gorged on redcurrants, raspberries,
strawberries, and, from the poultry yard, chicken.
With the coming war the visits stopped. In 1919,
Chernokolodez, the home with the sandpit outside
the kitchen window for cleaning and shining the
brass dishes, was seized by the red army. Stepan's
parents were arrested, and Stepan himself fled south
toward the Black Sea.

Two years later, after Ermolai quit the Petrograd
cadets, he went looking for Stepan and found him in
Dyushambe, where he had joined a resistance group.
They put a rifle in Ermolai's hands, and the two spent
the next four years together fighting with different
militias, alternately skirmishing with and running
from the Bolshevik invaders. It was clear to everyone
that the country was headed down the wrong path.
Support for the resistance was strong, if covert.
Ermolai wasn't much of a soldier—he could use a
guitar better than a rifle—and fought only because
he adored Stepan. Evenings when they were in the
field, they shared rations while Ermolai played the

songs he'd learned from his mother.

The night before his death, they were camped under a cliff overhang. The snow billowed and flakes coated the soldiers' heads white. These were men with whom Ermolai had shared meals and gotten drunk, wept and argued, slept and fought beside. Stepan, lost in contemplation, began humming a familiar melody, and Ermolai—who'd carried his guitar, cracked and scarred, into the mountains—picked up the tune. He sat close to the small fire so that his fingers wouldn't stiffen. In a hushed voice Stepan breathed the lyrics into the wind:

> *Through the sky a storm is sweeping,*
> *Whipping snowy whirlwinds around;*
> *It resembles childish weeping,*
> *Or a wild beast's wailing sound.*

At other times, before they knew of the Pamirs, when the vodka flowed freely, Ermolai would strike a bright chord and Stepan would break out in a voice that brought the blood rushing to all their faces and made everyone's stomach light:

> *So louder, oh music, sound the victory!*
> *Our foe's on the run, and we're victorious—*

Here the voices would pause until someone with enough drink in him fetched up the line in everyone's mind—"So, for the Tsar!"—then men would leap to their feet and bellow the outlawed national hymn that meant death for those caught singing it. Tears, arms around each other, shouts of joy for the

"White Dream!"—the cry for legitimate order, for law, for Russia—followed as they chanted "Huzzah! Huzzah! Huzzah!"

They were the remnants of a different country, a people who could imagine a world that changed through necessity, not force. Yet the White Dream persisted, because it was buoyed by the hopes of good people throughout the land.

❖ ❖ ❖

The seekers dig methodically with tiny axes. Water boils on nearby stoves. They've settled into small, precise movements, each working individually. They lack a soldier's vigor, and every so often one stops to gaze at the pewter sky or the white mountain before he shudders and returns to work. Ermolai knows they don't choose this place nor the cold. They can't feel the glacier's pulse. They work for other reasons.

Yesterday they unearthed Nikolai Charnota's corpse, just inside where the cave mouth had been. He wore the same greatcoat in which he died, and his body was preserved well though his face was frozen in a grimace that he never wore in life. The diggers pointed excitedly to the dark blossoms on his chest. Ermolai realized that they were trying to recreate the events of that distant afternoon. They wasted no time wrapping Nikolai's remains in a metallic blanket and packing them off to one of their shelters. Yet the real discovery awaits.

❖ ❖ ❖

Ermolai sat aloof on a boulder outside the cave. Below, the red soldiers took up positions. They fixed their rifles and the *tachanka*'s dark eye on the cave. The point between his eyes felt ticklish, and his empty stomach floated into his chest, fluttery and weak. While he wanted to feel grief, he couldn't. Stepan's suffering was finished. His sudden exit had left Ermolai alone, with frozen feet and hands, to count the blued barrels of enemy rifles.

"Come away from there," Nikolai said, but Ermolai paid no mind. Sitting in plain sight was a way of spitting in fate's eye.

A group of five red commissars trudged up the hill. The late afternoon sun dipped below the clouds and cast its light on the slope, stretching their shadows uphill. They called for the commanding officer, and Colonel Sorotov stepped out onto the ledge. Ermolai listened half-heartedly as the two sides shouted a truce, the commissars offering terms for surrender. Colonel Sorotov retreated into the cave and discussed with the remaining officers. There's no point in provoking certain death, they said to one another. We're outnumbered and outgunned. We're frozen and hungry. The only real option is surrender.

Ermolai thought of the suffering the reds had inflicted on the people, those in whose name they proclaimed to fight. What they did to professed enemies, who'd forced them to hike for weeks through ice-choked mountains, would certainly be worse.

His fellow soldiers began stuffing supplies into their packs, hiding knives and bread. Ermolai remained on the ledge.

"You should prepare," Nikolai called.

"Why? My toes are frozen. I can't move."

"The reds won't cut us any slack." Nikolai approached, and the roof's shadow bisected his face.

"I can't move," Ermolai said.

"Are you injured?"

"Why has all this happened? What does it mean?" Their band of white soldiers was one of the last pockets of resistance; they were being hunted to extinction.

"God will preserve us and we'll fight again in a different time and place."

"Don't give me that. Somehow things have gone terribly wrong. I'm only here because of Stepan." He looked at Nikolai, whose breath formed golden clouds in the sun's waning rays.

That's when a shriek cut the air. Inside the cave, men scattered as something hulking and white rushed past from the depths. Two men collapsed like dolls at its feet. Cries echoed. Below, shouts of "Look sharp!" and "Take aim!" rang out. Bullets lanced the air. Ice chunks stung Ermolai's cheeks. He couldn't tell who was firing. An arm's length away, Nikolai convulsed as if struck by invisible punches. Then the bullet, the one that took Ermolai's life, plowed into his side. He fell and came to rest under an ice shelf. The other soldiers ran onto the ledge, their arms fanning the air in surrender. The machine gun belched. It cut

down the men and poured bullets into the cave. Slabs
sheared from the walls. Then the mountain heaved
as if taking a slow inhalation, and the cave imploded.

Air emptied over Ermolai. It carried with it the
reek of curdled milk. There, stumbling under the ice
and snow cascading over its shoulders, stood the
beast. It fixed its gaze on Ermolai, and in its red-
rimmed liquid eyes he saw something unmistakable:
fear. It struck Ermolai then that they were *all* being
cheated. Fate was laughing in their faces, mocking
their cause, finishing them off in grand style. Then
the creature fell, and the ice buried it. The gunfire
stopped. The glacier groaned. Blood pulsed warmly
from between Ermolai's fingers. That's when he made
the vow: in death he would resist fate's mockery by
resisting fate itself.

❖ ❖ ❖

Again the seekers have found something—a black
vein in the layers of white, an ossified ember of a long-
dead fire around which Ermolai once sat as the frozen
ground turned red. Heat thawed his feet and hands.
He peeled off wool mittens to reveal fingers as black
as coal from the grave-digger's ax. It didn't matter.

The fire glowed against the mound of snow underneath which lay his companions. He pictured the
apartment where he grew up and the living-room
piechka, where the family gathered on winter nights
before the war, its tiles giving off such luxuriant heat.
As a boy, falling asleep, he'd listen to his mother
tell stories of Baba Yaga, Red Koko, and Vasilissa

the Beautiful. But that night on the glacier, it was Ermolai who was compelled to tell a story. He was the sole surviving white soldier, and the reds wanted an explanation. From their inferior position on the slope, the ledge had blocked their view inside the cave. There was no point in torturing the information out of him; he was in enough pain. It was only a matter of breathing slow enough so that he could speak. Their doctor examined his wounds, pronounced him finished, and gave him some warm tea for his final minutes.

To his surprise, after he finished his story they didn't shoot him, only made him show them where he last saw the beast. Then they left him alone. His gaze fell on a young soldier whose face flickered in the firelight. Why should one live and not the other? Why should this be the day that the White Dream died?

As the embers darkened, Ermolai began to feel a tugging in many directions and his thoughts turned to eternity. His father described it once: he said to imagine a steel ball the size of the earth then to picture that every century, a sparrow flies by and brushes the ball with its wing. By the time the sparrow has worn the ball into nothing, he said, eternity will not even have begun. As a boy, Ermolai took this to be some childish way of explaining things, but as the pins of the universe, like points on an escaping sphere, pulled at him, his father's face — the face he'd known and worshipped as a boy — returned. He imagined his father's whiskers, their scrape against his face when they kissed good night. When was the last time they'd kissed in such a way? He saw the thinning gray hair, the crooked nose, the scar above his eye. With that face in mind, Ermolai resisted. It's not difficult to resist, it's merely a breaking-off. He chose to leave the body but to persist in spirit. He would await the triumph of justice.

❖ ❖ ❖

The seekers have wasted two days excavating the wrong area. Since uncovering the fire, they've found only mushroomed slugs. They're digging inside where the cave was, and their faces are long, their hands tired and wambling. Once or twice a day the leader will walk out to the ledge, where Ermolai stands as a monument over the beast's corpse. He pauses as if listening to the wind, and Ermolai touches his face, caresses it, brushes with his thumb the V-shaped vein on the man's forehead. How beautiful the human face, he thinks. And how rugged the cold makes it, frost sprouting from beard and eyebrows, eyes becoming darker, skin ruddier, lips hardened. The cold has drawn out his inner man.

In the last moments before Ermolai's transformation, the reds dug three meters inside the cave's entrance, the spot he'd shown them.

"Mother of Mary," one of them said. The others gathered around. They dug deeper, then a dozen men hauled the corpse from the packed ice.

Its pink face was most like a man's, with pale blue eyes and finely crafted ears, expressive wrinkles around its mouth and worry creases frozen on its forehead.

Its elongated nose, uncannily humanlike, ended in flared nostrils. Hoary fur covered its body. It was terror draped in innocence, a cross between a man and a white bear. The doctor took measurements, then said he wanted to bring it with them out of the mountains. The men grumbled. It weighed as much as a horse. Who would carry it? The doctor offered instead to skin it, but the men still whispered. Bad luck, they said. Invited the evil eye. Just look what happened to the white soldiers. The head commissar gazed at the corpse for several minutes then shook his head.

"Write your report to General Topilskii," he said. "Then rebury it."

The next morning they dug a meter-deep hole on the ledge and dragged the corpse into it. Ice chunks pelted it from all sides as if the soldiers thought that even in death it deserved stoning. Then they swarmed over the ridge, hauling the *tachanka*, and hiked back the way they had come. Ermolai knew they would tell the story of what they'd seen.

III.

Months of research at various sites in the Pamirs failed to turn up any positive evidence.
GREAT SOVIET ENCYCLOPEDIA, "PRONIN"

Such a long wait. The seekers are close but they grow weary. It's late afternoon and their movements have slowed. They'll soon leave without that for which they came, and Ermolai will again be alone. The endless stretching of time seems unbearable. His existence is pointless if the beast's corpse goes undiscovered. The waiting will be for nothing.

You must look here, Ermolai cries.

The leader turns as if a frosted whisper had fallen on his ears. He walks to the ledge, stares straight at Ermolai, swipes the air as if testing the wind's strength. A shear of sunlight breaks from the clouds and coats the slope below in orange.

The leader calls the men over, motions to the ledge. They're reluctant. One of them drives a thin rod, hand-over-hand, into the ice. He shakes his head and turns away. The leader paces, then stops and stares at the ground. The others ponder the sky, which is pocked with purple clouds. The leader's yellow eyes blaze. He exhorts them to dig. They look to the distance. He kicks ice shards into the air. They begin collapsing the shelters. He thrashes the air with his arms as if the wind is blowing him off-balance. Ermolai falls to his knees and digs, but his hands pass through the snow, registering none of the cold and leaving no trace.

He continues to paw the snow. He feels as weak as a newborn. Pink streaks hatch the lavender sky as the last figure, the leader, pauses to glance back, then he too disappears over the ridge. The seekers' visit came and went so fast, the attempt so brief, it seems not to have happened.

As light fades and stars salt the sky, even the energy to remember who he is and why he was waiting seeps mercifully away from Ermolai. The second transformation is at hand. He awaits the downward gathering pull, but it doesn't come.

He realizes with flukish disappointment that he has miscalculated. There'll be no final journey into the glacier. He won't pass through the beast's body, feel its frozen flesh, nor through the cold-hardened capillaries of ambered resin from long-dead trees, the petrified honeycombs buried in dark-ored veins, the frozen soil, the deep pools of water with crystallized threads of ice reaching like roots into them. What overtakes him is the opposite: expansion, dissipation, divergence, a radiating of particles, those he thought of as himself and himself one of countless others, each a singular speck guided in some larger and more complete dispersal. There's time to mourn the loss of what he's known, but he foregoes it, casts it off like a shell, and instead turns outward, eager to explore all that's been gained.

❖

THE RUNCITER PROJECT

CLAIRE'S TEARS

One day last fall while Gerald Runciter was dying, his daughter Claire descended the stairs to my sunken apartment, knocked on the door, and held out a crumbling cardboard box. Through its cracked sides sprung budding glimpses of loose-leaf papers and the curled corners of notebooks. In it, she said, were her father's personal research and writings. She suspected that it contained a great oeuvre, something that would preserve his genius once and for all and something that I could recognize best since we shared so many interests and were so close. She didn't want to wait until he was gone to pass them along—that seemed somehow too sad. I tendered the box against a hip. The first yellow spots were blooming like melanomas on the elm leaves in the front yard. She asked me once again with her eyes, and after a fluttering moment of indecision, I agreed, promising to do everything in my power to honor her father's memory.

For a month while Gerald lay embrowning in hospice, I agonized over those mail scraps, napkin notes, three annotated paperbacks, and eleven cloth-bound journals, fretting how to bring him back to life though he had yet to finish dying. I've trained myself to be a man not easily moved by others' feelings, but Claire's tears beleaguered me. Besides showing why dormant emotions ought to be frequently exercised in order to temper their force, her tears were a haunting reminder that it had fallen to me to solidify my lover's legacy. Mornings I'd sit and watch him waste away, trying not to stare at his naked face, his raccoon eyes, his cheekbones stretching his caramelized skin so taut that it glistened. If he looked uncomfortable, I'd adjust the pitch of his bed then fluff his pillows. Afternoons I'd hole up in my apartment and pore over the box's artifacts.

Runciter's hand was an imbrication of cramped squarish letters that collided with one another and borrowed limbs to the point of illegibility—and when I *could* decipher it, the writing turned out to be tedious and impersonal. This couldn't be the result of poor writing facilities. Unlike this room that I pay for by the week in the outskirts of a forlorn city, the place where Gerald worked before he took sick was a spacious study in his house on Q Street in Port Angeles, Washington: book-lined walls, beechwood desk, rolling drink cart, and a window overlooking his cockles and tomato plants. On languid after-noons sunlight angled across the study and lamped a universe of rudderless dust motes.

Though he'd been an electrical engineer by training, in retirement Runciter's interests widened. He used the journals to work out problems in fields ranging from philosophy to pharmaceuticals to animal husbandry. His method was disorderly: in order to explore a concept—say, zebra copulation—he rolled it around on the page like the surf tosses a log; however, there was never mention of the surge that propelled the driftwood answer ashore. Once achieving clarity and *before* recording the final (critical!) insight—in this case, how on earth they tell each other apart—he simply stopped writing. The resulting tangle and what I had to work with was like reading tea leaves, a skill my grandmother failed to pass along.

I despaired.

One night as I sat dewy-eyed, listening to "Nutbush City Limits" and sinking into depression, I surrendered. In the morning, I decided, I would confess my failure to Claire. A moment later, the universe interceded: a dead synapse fired and stirred a memory from the past summer, of pulling that numbing burn into my mouth as the air echoed with the cry of a quail separated from his covey. Gerald and I were sitting on his deck, freebasing his special blend and discussing the uses of books, when suddenly he recited Emerson in that lilting voice: "I had better never see a book than be warped by its attraction clean out of my own orbit and made a satellite instead of a system." As he said this, two strings of blue smoke fell from his nostrils.

I jumped up and slapped the ceiling. The depression vanished. I'd been looking at Runciter's writings as if they were snapshots of an essential truth. My mistake had been confining myself to a system of his design, worshiping *his* past instead of *my* future. I was performing archeology instead of art! Immediately after it was gone, I sensed that something had been constraining me, something erstwhile, and I vowed to recommit myself to the Runciter project along a new direction, one founded stubbornly on my own freedom. It was the best and only way forward, and in order to cement the resolution, I rushed to the hospice.

As serendipity would have it, this was the same night that Gerald passed. All the same, the conviction endured and, along with what I know of his character and habits, fueled the encomium you now hold.

Enclosed are only the most vital organs from Runciter's body of private writings, culled, trimmed, and divided into four sections for easy consumption. Despite the bellyaching that'll no doubt occur, the commentary avoids the Boswellian trap so many biographers fall into. Instead, it uses Runciter's ideas as pools, pockets, bright beams of light, nature's bulls-eyes—*alain lumity* the Persians called them—into which I bore with fullest force, deepening the points made visible by fate having selected him for an early thump and leaving me the liberty to press ahead. With a final glance over my shoulder at the fugacious past, I look to tomorrow. After all, my eyes are set in my forehead.

Yakiv Zharko
The Jerkwater Outskirts of
America's Most Nondescript City
January 5, 2015

❖❖❖

The Devil's Dandruff

From Artifact 10, penciled on a green sticky note:
QA141.2 M32

At the Clallam County Public Library I found the referenced book: *Number Words and Number Symbols* by Karl Menninger. Its yellowed pages gasped as if for breath, exhaling as they did figures of Kai Island marriage tablets, Roman denarii, Egyptian pictographs, and Philippine swords inlaid with silver nails as kill marks. Studying the images brought to mind a section of the journals. On pages 43–52 of what I've labeled "Journal A," Runciter considers a particular phenomenon he alternately describes as "vestiges," "projections," "illuminations," and, later, "fragments." His working technical definition appears on page 50:

> *It's well known that F'Abrám's cortical scale, associating event-related action potentials attributed to integral stimuli with regions in the cerebrum—as understood at the present time—when applied to particular classes of stimulants, leads to asymmetries which do not appear to be inherent in the phenomena—*

Do you appreciate my difficulties now?? To say that Runciter lacked a velvet touch with language is to use a single bristle when what's wanted is a mop; yet a

little digging uncovers true insight. What our word-
smith claims on page 50 in Journal A is that we ought
to reconsider a particularly neglected relationship,
namely that between *Ach sapiens* and integers—and,
later, his real breakthrough: that numbers themselves
might very well have agency(!).

From Artifact 14, a chamber of commerce pamphlet:
*When out traveling in beautiful Clallam County, don't
forget to enjoy the local flavor that you find pleasurable.*

Is serendipity the same as synchronicity? The first
time I met Gerald was at the opening for his exhibit
at the Hugin and Munin Art Gallery in downtown
Port Angeles. I'd happened across the notice in the
newspaper and made the trip over from the city. The
place was airy and bright. Though I was early, several
bottles of cheap merlot had already been uncorked
and placed beside an uninspired cheese array. On the
wall hung the fluidic nimbus of a maple leaf I was
studying when someone behind me cleared his throat.
I turned and there stood a serious man, somewhere
in his late fifties, in a pinstripe suit. He had bushy
gray whiskers and fluffy eyebrows. He looked surprisingly fit, with well-shaped round cheekbones and
a rippled brow. A ruby the size of a marble glinted
from a thumb ring, but what struck me most were his
eyes, which floated like two desert islands high in his
forehead and were no color at all—no more gray than
blue, no more green than brown. They passed lightly

over me as he introduced himself as the artist then said something about devil's dandruff, the drug war, and coca eradication. I laughed. And those islands welcomed me onto their shores.

My mouth went oven-dry. My palms iced over. When he offered me a glass of wine, I accepted. Cheese, yes. More wine, thank you. When I told him who my grandfather was, he flushed with pleasure. It felt like I was burning and floating at the same time. Somehow the conversation veered to my appearance, and he said that my wife was a very lucky woman.

"I've been fortunate enough not to acquire one of those," I said.

"Oh?" He lifted an eyebrow. Then someone called him away, but before he left he said, "Don't leave without saying goodbye."

Soon the gallery filled with the predictable assortment of folks, poseur epicures and small-fish collectors, all clamoring for his attention. As I made for the door, he broke away from a trio of gray hairs and pressed a card into my hand. He said to call him, we could have coffee and discuss electrophotography. I expected that the sparks would soon subside. After all, he was easily thirty years older and too somber for my taste. As I came to find, though, I couldn't stop thinking about the man in the pinstripe suit.

From the back of a drugstore receipt: *It was Pherecydes who first suggested that it might be possible to weigh the human soul.*

This is one of the few points of clear connection
between the man I knew and his work. In Journal D
he spends ten pages contemplating an 1862 study by
Samuel Skanson, a doctor who used silk sheets and
extremely sensitive scales to weigh terminal patients.
Skanson found that the average patient loses 0.23
ounces at the moment of death.

The first time I visited Gerald at his house, a week
after the exhibit opening, he spoke of Skanson's work.
At the time, I thought he was simply trying to prove
that his knowledge was broad-ranging and that he
wasn't only interested in me for my body and my family
connections. We sat on his deck sipping Madeira. He
produced a tiny packet, the kind KFC used to put
in their meal amenities package along with a napkin,
spork, and wet wipe, and held it up like he was dis-
playing a new stamp. Then he tossed it into my lap.

"What's this?"

"One-fifth of an ounce of salt."

I pinched the package and gauged its heft. An
arousing tickle awoke in my lower belly: a sensation
that I came to associate with Gerald's presence. It
was as if a fruit fly had crawled between the teeth of
my pants zipper and was happily buzzing away.

"Not much, is it?" I said. The twin paper capsules
contained maybe seventy-five salt grains apiece. It felt
like nothing, like a Tic-Tac, a tissue, a movie ticket.

"If our internal electrical energy, like light, has
mass—and why shouldn't it?—then what Skanson
found might be the weight of the life-force itself,
don't you think?"

"I can already picture the new fad diet: lose weight now, shed your soul."

"Your grandfather would've found this interesting."

I wanted badly to say something impressive, so I settled on what I hoped was an oversight. "It's probably just the air leftover in the lungs."

"Hah," he said and wagged a hairy finger. "Lung air weighs far less than a quarter-ounce, even if the lobes are full. I worked out the proof yesterday."

Indeed, it's this formula that appears on page 32 of Journal D.

The desire to say something significant persisted; the worst thing is being judged vapid. But nothing—nothing!—came to mind.

"The point is," Gerald Runciter finally said, "death is merely a reapportioning of energy. The worms and grubs, et cetera, take care of the physical, but what's left of the energy that electrophotography so clearly captures? What your grandfather and I have unveiled, I suggest, may very well be the soul itself."

Later that afternoon, with Gerald's coaching, I freebased coke for the first time. It was a special mix he'd perfected himself, made from a pink crystal the size of a fingernail. He became almost boyish in his eagerness to show me where he kept them: in a five-sided wooden box that he hid from his wife in the false bottom of a desk drawer that only opened with the magnetic key embedded under the ruby on his right thumb. One thing led to another and before long we were drowning in kisses. Gone was Grandpa Runciter; before me was a very alive Gerald!

Of course I should've seen that what he was offering wasn't love; he was manipulative, hypocritical, and self-serving. But that night was bliss. To top it off, as I drifted into hypnagogic sleep, I entered for the first time a plane of an entirely different order.

The moment I write of—on the cusp of sleep—brimmed with vitality and strangeness. Everything shone with such crystal clarity, for lack of a more hyperbolic (and still inadequate) term, that it simply overwhelmed. I suppose my shell of a body remained in Gerald's arms, but that core feeling of knowing who I was transformed completely. What I saw, what I *became*, were various universal fragments, a gamboling stream that seemed to have always existed just outside of conscious perception. And it all felt so natural, so matter-of-fact: it was the discovery of a neighborhood that had been bustling away for years just around a corner I'd never turned.

The various worlds rushed forward, collapsed, and reconfigured. And each shocked with its immediacy. At once I was the rust-freckled prow of a ship unseaming the ocean, a world that held for several moments before it kaleidoscopically transformed (I became a sort of roving, sensate eyeball) into a cottonwood seed floating past the mouth of a limestone cave, a world from which I again morphed, this time into a glint of sun on the side of a shiny black ashtray on a coffee table in the back room of a warehouse, a scene that dissolved and resolved, once again, so that I became a filet knife deboning a soft leather scabbard, the latter going limp by inches—and the inhabiting continued with each new world crowding out the former.

When I slowed down to pinpoint my initial reaction to a single fragment, I found it to be astonished repulsion because each was so *different*. It violated the previous vision so powerfully that it caused a total and instantaneous rearrangement, but it was the shock of this very repulsion that allowed the violation to become the new order—and all that appeared prior, an aberration. If this were the extent of the experience, a sort of jumpy hyper-vivid dream, it could've been filed away as unusual but in no way remarkable. What made it so compelling were the emotional links that formed along the way. Each new world arrived so suddenly that I felt frantic at all that had just been lost, realizing that the former fragment's majesty was gone forever. But as the new world blossomed, the sense of loss edged into fresh exhilaration. By the end of each fragment, I had been won over, lifted into blissful harmony, and perched again for devastation.

The overall result carried such powerful sensations— abject despondency and sweeping grandiosity—that, upon reflection, it seemed a person could give his whole life for such sequential stimulation. I imagined that the only thing comparable might be if a person had no concept of the ocean or waves and then found himself in open water during a storm, each trough a watery grave, each crest an expansive height. It was life upon life upon life, with death thrown in as well.

Waking brought with it a compulsion to record everything witnessed, a yearning so strong that it drove me to spend the next day locked away madly scribbling all that I could remember. I reached for details. The fragments' features faded with time, so this rendered my efforts a race against loss. If I were a visual artist, I would've painted a mass of bright scenes raining down one atop another, but journaling was the only way that I had to exercise the wonderful, haunting visions.

❖ ❖ ❖

ONE MAN'S LIFE

From a passage marginally double-lined in Runciter's paperback copy of *A Poem In Four Cantos*:

> *Just this: not text, but texture; not the dream*
>
> *But topsy-turvical coincidence,*
>
> *Not flimsy nonsense, but a web of sense.*

I've always been a very impressionable man. For this reason I avoid reading medical books and diagnostic manuals. I had to learn this about myself the hard way: while reading a graphic novel about one man's life with Crohn's Disease, when the ileum becomes inflamed, especially during periods of high stress and anxiety, I lost weight and developed arthritic-like pain, diarrhea, and itchy eyes. One day during this period, I was in line at my favorite coffee shop, where a certain barista cupped his hand over the espresso tamper in a way that set the fruit fly buzzing in my underwear. This barista, this Carl, had a face that burned with such intensity that I had to shy away as if from the sun. While Gerald was sick, I built all sorts of fantasies about introducing Carl to the fragments, then running off together to some faraway place where we'd have them all to ourselves, lounging on king-size hotel beds and describing our journeys with them to each other. There Carl was, forming a puck under the gurgle of the machine, and I'd just gathered the nerve to say more than my usual, "Tall nonfat extra-dry cappuccino," when my stomach revolted. It felt as if I had swallowed lighter fluid and followed it with a lit match. Though my heart frenzied, when Carl stepped to the register to take my order, I acted as if nothing was wrong. I never did find out what time he got off work.

From Journal G, page 41: *In my research, one idea in particular resonates—that suggested by Lazlo F'Abrám...*

I've been unable to locate F'Abrám's work. No electronic records of it or of him exist. What we have is Runciter's secondhand paraphrase, which can be summarized: F'Abrám claims that certain thinkers throughout history (Pythagoras, Jesus, the Buddha, Muhammad, Galileo, and so on) have tapped into a universal structure, a network of relations that surrounds and upholds our reality, a scaffold for the cosmos, something Plato called *aither* and Aristotle called *quintessence*. Five is the key, it turns out. Were I not afraid of being labeled "unstable"—or worse, an "overreaching artist"—I'd outright claim that a fragment is a transmission along this invisible network.

Passage underlined in a hardback by Stanislas Dehaene: *Our best system of axioms fails to capture, in a unique way, our intuitions of what numbers are.*

If pressed, I could find traces of my impressionability in childhood. It manifested as a certain receptivity to the world, which I saw in the patterns around me. For instance, when I was as young as two, I would stare into my mother's coffee cup at a trio of dark lines on the china, perceiving a pattern that, expressed numerically, would read 1-2-3; 3-2-1; 1-3-2; 2-3-1; 2-1-3; 3-1-2. This was well before I learned to count, so I perceived each integer not as a number but as an acute touch sensation. The pattern imposed itself onto me from the outside; of this I've always been certain. Growing up, I found the world, not to mention my body—fingers, limbs, two eyes, that sometimes flaccid, sometimes stout Numero Uno between my legs—to be teeming with complex and ever more intricate imbrications: 5, 14, 23, 32, et cetera—but somewhere along the stormy path of adolescence, any predilection for numerical intimacy, like so much of childhood, was blown into the ether like playing cards swept up by a mistral wind.

From Artifact 32, a hospice brochure: ...*we offer a tranquil atmosphere...*

Our "eternal love" (G. Runciter, 10 June 2014, Four Winds Hotel, Room #207) lasted a grand total of five weeks. During that time I moved from Seattle to Port Angeles and we began meeting at the apartment that I rented across from the airport, and at hotels. Also, Gerald's wife took three overnight trips that summer, and I stayed at his house twice while she was away.

Upon Gerald's request, I brought my grandfather's originals. They were my sole inheritance after my parents perished in a house fire when I was fourteen. The disaster occurred shortly after we immigrated from Ukraine to the West Coast. As a child I had trouble sleeping. Various soporifics worked but caused strange effects. I was sleepwalking in the yard when the boarding house we were staying in erupted in red flames. The house fell away in black sheets. My parents had stored the photos in a safe deposit box, and they became the only thing saved from my life with them. All of my Ukrainian relatives were rogues and criminals, so I entered the court system, keeping my grandfather's originals with me wherever I moved: 75 matted 8 x 12 photographs. When despair crept up, as it so often did, I would slide them from their double-padded folder and run my fingertips along their brilliant patterns of light.

That summer, Gerald and I fell into a pleasant routine. Always there was Madeira and palavering; always the pink crystal; always love; and at the end of the night, always the fragments. Often the next morning it felt as if Gerald was watching me, on the verge of asking something, but we never spoke about them. I regret that now very much, since I found in his journals that he'd tapped into them long before.

From Artifact 14, a Pritchard Art Gallery advertisement: ...*electrophotography*...

Nicola Tesla was the first to try aural photography, but he soon dropped it for other pursuits. A Brazilian priest built a camera and made the first images of a scintillating energy network never before seen. Imagine Father Moura in the cloistered quarters of a Porto Alegre monastery, hunched over a makeshift voltage generator, a stack of emulsified metal plates at elbow. The Church, of course, unable to see past its eternally-stunted nose, confiscated his equipment and destroyed the priceless images. They deemed the work to be in doctrinal conflict.

Little did they know that my Grandfather Semyon would refine Moura's camera and record ground-breaking images of the light-filled penumbras and channels that reside within and around all living beings. As a boy I would visit his studio and for hours stare at the images of palms, fingers, rats, kittens, apples, tomatoes—all effused with magical light. The leaves' coronas fascinated me most, bristling with their fiery silhouettes, their veins merely sleeves for the tentacles of dazzling promise within. My grandfather called them "fields of life" and claimed that some day they would change medicine (for years the Russians have used them on their athletes to detect sources of stress). In two separate studies, he even observed these networks in organic matter for up to three days after death; ironic, isn't it, that this fits so well with Church doctrine, since it provides scientific backing for that mystery of life within death — for resurrection within the precise demands exacted by a biblical timeframe.

From Journal K, page 23: *FUCK!*

It's very simple. This was the night, June 26, that everything changed. That witch with a capital B went as white as porcelain the first time I saw her in person, which was the same moment she entered her bedroom, back early from a trip to Anacortes, and found her husband asleep with his arm draped over me. Because I was already awake, staring into space, plotting how to record that night's tantalizing fragments, I saw her horror turn almost immediately to cold cunning as the alimonied dollar signs flashed in her eyes. She threw the predictable fit, I was hurried into my clothes, and Gerald stopped answering the phone.

From Journal K, page 32: *If only [the fragments] would return!*

By this point, which I estimate to be sixty-eight days before his demise, Gerald was sorely missing the nightly stream. The numbers we had managed to contact had grown fickle. Their transmissions must've stopped for him the same as they had for me, even though he still had the customized coke. It's not hard to imagine his preparations: the knotted stomach, the superciliary tension, the cottony mouth—all deterrents to receiving. Perhaps his deteriorating physical condition further stymied his access. Like me, he must've longed to be reconnected.

I phoned on a Friday night during this period to invite him out for some carousing. By then his wife had been gone for several weeks so he'd started answering again.

"Oh, it's you," he said. "Thank God there're no handguns in my house."

"What's that supposed to mean?"

"No stout ropes and lofty rafters. No straight-edged razors. No economy-size jars of acetaminophen—"

"Don't be stupid," I said.

"—no ergot, no vehicles without airbags, no garrotes and spoons. I'm going to tell you some bad news. I'm sick, Yak. The Big C."

"The Big C?"

"You wouldn't understand," he said and hung up. That was the last healthy conversation we had.

From a note inside the back cover of a paperback
copy of *Wieland: The night I lost [the fragments]
was due to a stupid mistake. Oh God, why me?!
Decades wasted...*

The hospice room where Gerald died was a decent
affair—a bit cramped but in a way described as
"intimate" in their advertising. Alternating shades of
beige served as the color scheme. Warm landscapes
of moose and snow-capped peaks decorated the walls.
A picture window framed the edge of a newly planted
forest. For nearly a week Runciter had been semi-con-
scious. I had just arrived in something of a rush when,
on this particular afternoon, he surfaced. Claire ran
for a nurse. He fixed me with a gaze, his colorless
eyes staring from over the top of his oxygen mask.
He still wore the ruby ring. Thinking that I might not
get another chance, I asked about where he might've
recorded the special formula in his journals, but he
kept silent. Then a voice I didn't recognize crackled out.

"I want to be buried," it said.

"Come again?"

"Claire has ideas," Runciter said, then swirled the
air by his ear with the heart-rate monitor taped to
his finger. "She wants to incinerate me, but Yakiv...
will you *bury* me?"

What a proposal! My heart still shudders. His
emphasis on the word "bury" was unmistakable, and
his eyes burned with such intensity that I could only
whisper, "Yes." Then his face eclipsed and his eyelids
dropped. Curtains, I thought.

Those words—what ended up being his last wish (and *how*, I ask, should I be expected simply to ignore a dying lover's last wish?)—echoed in my head. I knew that Claire had arranged for cremation so this meant unmaking her plans. I took his hand. He had worn the thumb ring for so long that the bone had grown around it like xylem vessels around a wire. I must've been so shaken that I gripped his shoulders, urging him to reawaken and clarify, perhaps even retract, this terrible responsibility that he had thrust on me. A rasp crossed his lips, so I peeled away the mask and cupped my hands around his mouth as an amplifier for any final message. That's when that nurse barged in and found me leaning over my friend even as his soul's quarter-ounce slipped through my fingers.

❖ ❖

THE BOX

From Journal K, page 5: *In this dream I found the dilemma presented in crystal-clear terms—Thanatos and Eros clashing in a never-ending battle.*

A pounding startled me awake this morning. My first impulse was to bolt out a window, but I saw through the peephole that it was only Claire.

"I want my father's box back," she said.

I could tell by the edge in her voice that she was donning the role of spurned ingénue and had finally bought into the deluded nurse's story. I pleaded with her that I was on the threshold of tying everything together in a transcendent dénouement. She said that she was cleaning out her father's house. After it sold she planned to return to her life in Philadelphia.

So I tried the direct route.

"Do you know how much it costs to post bail when you're under suspicion of voluntary manslaughter? I had to hock my grandfather's entire collection."

"Look, I'm sorry for your troubles," she said. "But I really need my dad's stuff back."

So there I was, wondering if she was still planning cremation and how I was going to make good on my promise to Gerald for an earthly burial. I didn't want to raise her suspicion about my intent, so even though I had made only a few pages of notes, I handed over, in all its crumpled glory, the box, thinking, like alpha and omega, each time Claire stood on my doorstep that it signified something larger.

"You know, Yakiv, I don't think you killed my father. After all, he was dying. Why would you do such a thing?" She sleeved tears from her cheeks. The elm tree's leaves were gone, and its black skeleton rose up stark and eerie, the template ready to mint a warehouse of gallows trees.

"I loved your father."

"I know. That's why I let you have these. But now I need them back."

"If you trusted me, you'd let me keep them."

She scrunched one side of her face as if she'd been stabbed in the side. "You know, I think my mother was right about you after all. You really are disturbed."

With that she climbed the stairs, the worn heels of her tennis shoes the last I saw of her.

I slumped into a chair. Not only had my lover just died and not only was I accused of offing him, but now I'd been robbed of any hope of reconnecting with the fragments. My whole uninspiring life rose up around me like a pit. I wondered if sunken despair was to be my new state of residence.

From Journal K, pages 38-39: *When night falls, a weight descends. Activities that never before failed to excite hold no appeal. I stop films two-thirds of the way through—even at the climax I cut them off. Their normal power holds no sway. I prefer the characters to stay trapped in the predicaments of caving-in lives. I'm not interested in the well-crafted solution that extracts them from their situation, only the down-tending crisis.*

Do you see how Runciter and I mirrored each other, shared precisely the same emotional states, were moieties of the same whole? As I sat there in my apartment waiting for the authorities to come collect me, an idea struck like ideas so often do—when they're least expected and most needed. If I could acquire Gerald's corpse, I could bury him at his house and retrieve his special kit all at once, thus fulfilling two promises—one to him and one to myself—in a single stroke. I had always believed that the Zharko line was destined to fulfill a great purpose. Staring at my grandfather's images as a boy, I'd felt the approach

of a fate of extreme significance—and here it was
before me, the chance to do something more than
drape myself over the furniture and inhale Oreos.

Runciter's chemical catalyst opened the gateway
to another realm of knowledge. Depending upon
my actions over the next several hours, his discovery
would either persist or perish. The beechwood desk
would go to some nitwit junk collector in an estate
sale who'd never find the secret drawer and, if he did,
would never know the proper use of the pink crystals
inside the pentagonal box. The insight into the hidden
life of numbers rested solely with me.

What an onus!

Runciter had died the day before yesterday. His
mortal remains were reclining at mortuary. While in
hospice he had assigned clear inheritance of everything to Claire and chosen a columbarium slot (which,
when no one was around, I teased him was his "ash
hole"), epitaph font, pithy quote, et cetera. I quickly
gathered the proper paperwork, rental van, and a dark
suit. With those items it was no problem to get the
morgue to release his remains; it's not difficult to
duplicate crematoria stationary.

That's how, in the late afternoon of the third day
since Gerald's passing, I picked up what was left of
him and the two of us drove around until twilight.
When Claire's car finally left its spot on Q Street,
under a wintry sunset gleam, I maneuvered the van
down the driveway and onto the dirt path leading
through the back gate. My cold cappuccino sloshed
in its holder. The van sent its beam of sallow light

into the sprawling backyard and across the skeletal remnants of Runciter's tomato plants. Their rotting fruits sagged from yellow branches. I considered a green burial right there but at the last minute worried that fresh earthworks might attract raccoons. Since a backhoe was out of the question, a single possibility remained.

Concentrated potassium hydroxide is a nasty chemical. In preparation, I had purchased a cloth mask to veil my face and a zip-up suit made of impermeable white plastic with furbelowed cuffs. It was no gossamer gown but it would have to do. I dragged the body downstairs, the skull thudding on each step, the torso squirreling every which way. My blood was already rushing when the reek of rat nests and sodden dirt hit. At the bottom of the stairs, a caged bulb dangled from a cord, its light bouncing off the walls like camera flashes. A score of shiny brown capsules, chrysalides, hung from a trio of overhead boards, suspended by silken filaments. How they'd gotten into this dank hole was a mystery, but there they were, our gallery of witnesses.

I proceeded deeper into the mildew and filth. I had cut fresh flowers—roses and hollyhocks, johnny jump-ups and late-blooming irises—from the local arboretum. The bouquet trembled in my hands, in which I also clutched a pair of Japanese pruners. When I reached the appointed place with its candle-holder and tools, I kneeled and began what had to be done, this fulfillment of Runciter's last request, this bonding of our fates.

At some point, hands blistered from the earth work, legs and back stiff, sweat trickling down my sides, a realization struck: how does it happen that, at some point, you look around at the cramped confines of a crawlspace and realize that you're on your knees holding a short-handled shovel, digging a shallow grave by the smoky light of menorah candles, about to clip the thumb off of your ex-lover's corpse?

The heat and strain took their toll; I swooned.

From Journal K, page 14: *Surely joy is the condition of life, yet I feel none, only a wide pit opening under me. And there's no upward movement.*

I awoke to bare earth against my face, the air peppery with burnt wax and decay. My vision came into focus on the lump in the body bag made by Runciter's head.

What I did next surprised even me. I recall watching Runciter lie there cocooned in that zippered shell, the two of us in syzygy across that abyssal border, when, like those strange patterns that had pressed into my boyish mind as I stared into my mother's coffee cup, a sensation occurred, clear and visceral: of Gerald's brain still pulsing with fields of life. My grandfather and Runciter himself had recorded this blurring of extremes. The horrid days in mortuary! That stifling bag, the hours spent on the van's hard bed, the doors squealing open, the thud of being plopped onto the patio then clumped down the stairs. How unfeeling I had been. Empathy with the living, yes, but will you go a step further? As long as those electric fields coursed his brain's pleated neurons, Runciter was still connected to the universe. His soul persisted! I can only explain my action thus: that seemed like no condition in which to bury a former lover, even if he was a deadbeat.

You might imagine my mixed feelings at unzipping the body bag and cracking his corpse over the head with the shovel. I assure you that it was done purely and wholeheartedly out of a sense of mercy. What happened next changed me forever. A diaphanous light-blue light effloresced from the crown of his head and swept up into the air and curled over my forearms. It snaked around my torso and neck. It slid past my lips. Yes, I tell you that I swallowed Gerald's very soul. It tasted of sugar and lemons with a dash of salt. Then in a flash the side door creaked open and a shaft of light cut the darkness. I glanced up, expecting to see the beam of a police flashlight and Claire's pale forefinger.

But nothing. Only a scurrying of rats or mice or wolf spiders where the ground sloped toward the study's flooring, which supported that beechwood desk with its false compartment, and where, redolent of Cuban tobacco, lay that special box inside of which waited my Pyrrhic fragments of paradise.

❖❖❖

IN THE PURLIEUS

From the back of Artifact 32, a torn envelope: *There is no mng, only an alphabet in which u write your own mng*

You might think that this commentary runs the risk of affecting the world somehow, the world of the living. Rest assured that I'm a firm believer in the fluidity of names and genders, of denatured truth. Of course, if Claire reads this, she'll recognize the details and be reduced to tears. I can only advise her to take up drinking. Also, if she doesn't mind getting her hands dirty, she's welcome to disinter her father and light him up like a roman candle: I hope he burns with the intensity of the fragments.

You see, they've returned. I've perfected the heating process. Inhalation brings that blissful tingling in the gums followed by pure tranquility. And more: with practice, I've learned how to block out the swell and attune my thoughts to a single integer's transmission. Night after night the process repeats. I seduce and am seduced by a different number. Soon I hope to locate them on the number line, to pin each fragment to its name. You see, I've found, as mathematicians have long known, that each number does in fact brim with personality and something akin to existential pride.

Thank God for infinity!

So I witness and record, then obsessively revise, seeking always that initial thrill. What I'm pursuing is even grander than the medical application that my grandfather envisioned. In these months I've found a contentment knowing that I'm contributing to my bloodline's central work. The only thing that distracts me from my great purpose: the supply of specialized crystal is nearing its end. When it's gone, misery won't be far behind.

Until then I'm lurking in the purlieus of the city where, like Hieronymous Bosch and other maladjusted malcontents, I've chosen to live—an out-of-the-way, nearly forgotten place. It's on the edge of things, where solitude and anonymity operate, that I hope to honor the legacies of Runciter and my grandfather. If things go well, someday you'll see our handiwork.

❖

THE MYSTERIOUS
INTENSITY OF
THE HEART

An elephant felt it first. At 9:27 p.m., through the ten-inch concrete floor in the Pachyderm Habitat at the Denver Zoo, Olympia, a forty-four-year-old Asian elephant, detected the minute disturbances with the extremely sensitive array of Pacinian corpuscles that circumscribed her ivory-tipped toes. In her many years at the zoo, nothing like this had ever occurred. She felt afraid, for herself and the herd, so she trumpeted. Over and over. By the time the night attendant arrived, all five elephants were pacing their enclosures. She checked their giant water troughs: all full. She aimed a flashlight between their stone-gray legs, convinced that one of the free-roaming peacocks had snuck inside. Nothing. Again Olympia trumpeted. When things didn't settle down, the attendant phoned her supervisor, fearing, correctly, that things would only get worse.

The next day, the zoo was in uproar. The Amur tigers paced their cage, clawed the air, and complained

with fang-bearing roars. Mothers yanked children
from the glass and hurried to the next exhibit. The
Arabian camel, bolting in wild ellipses around its
outdoor pen, seeded a column of dust that climbed
into the sky. The red panda scaled high into its bamboo
branches. The Andean condor pumped out-of-use
wings and launched itself into the overhead netting.

The mother-son pair of mandrill baboons scam-
pered from ledge to ledge in their concrete room.
Eventually, Dil, the juvenile, bit Viv, who squealed
and ran to the corner and sat cringing. Cries rever-
berated, fear pheromones seeped through the vents,
the camel's dust rose, and all the while the tick-tock
rhythm itched away at Dil's finger pads. The attendants heard Viv's screams but were too late. By the
time they turned the hose on him he had already
killed her; she was the first casualty.

As the smoggy orange glow that was the sun inched
closer to the Rockies, shredded newspaper bits and
carpet fibers began to quiver. Dogs, cats, rabbits,
chinchillas, iguanas, frogs, and hissing cockroaches
hissed and croaked and squealed and yowled and
threw themselves against cage doors, lids, screens,
and fences. Finding escape, they raced down side-
walks and driveways, along streets, and across lawns
of Kentucky bluegrass in the tips of which they again
felt the terrible pulse: so they ran and crawled faster
until the rhythm existed only in memory, but even
there it overwhelmed the spell of complacency that,
as pets, the soothing human voices and hands had
cast over them, so they kept leaping and scraping

onward over fields and ditches into the foothills and onto the plains, spilling in a thousand directions away from the city.

In Ft. Collins the tremors tripped a seismic warning system that set off a chain of notifications. Just past midnight all along the Front Range, fighter jets and bombers were scrambled. They lifted off, rising sharp and banking hard until they became cogs in a giant wheel circumscribing the Mile High City, where thousands of people, having chased pets and searched neighborhoods and put up fliers and dried their children's eyes, went to bed and fell asleep, unaware of the tons of steel swimming in the night sky, watching over them and waiting.

❖ ❖ ❖

At six minutes past two in the morning, Maria Delgado was not one of the sleepers. Though she had been in Denver for less than five months, already she felt connected to the city and could sense that something was changing. That afternoon, her skin had registered a note of autumn coolness while walking home from the bus stop with Diana, her sister-in-law. They were always quiet on the walk and Maria cherished the time, listening to the sounds carried on the thin air—the distant drone of Federal Way, music trailing an open-windowed car, the calls of a child for its pet—while admiring the western mountains, a purple wall with caps gleaming white even at summer's end. She liked to imagine those blinding white fields of snow and ice. Hector had told her about the mountains. There's nothing like this in Aguascalientes, he said. These are *real* mountains. And wait until you see a sunset—they say if God's not a Broncos fan, then why are sunsets orange and blue?

Hector's snores tickled her neck, his jaw shelved on her shoulder. The bed was so small that they had to spoon all night, and when one of them turned over the other had to follow. She could just make out the soft respirations of their nieces, six and four years old, asleep across the room. Through the open window the lilacs rustled. Again, something new: all summer there'd been no wind, but these small gusts came with the freshness of a just-opened freezer. She attuned herself to the wind's journey, convinced she caught whiffs of Pacific salt and desert sand, hints of lemons and apples from western-slope orchards, the chill of glaciered mountain peaks, and the dampness of air trundling down through whitewater canyons.

Maria shifted, felt the soreness in her lower back. She hated the motel. Earlier that day, the boss had caught her. She was just about to swat a fly in the room that she was cleaning. It was perched on a yellow jacket carcass in the windowsill, knitting the air, when masses of milky white banana-shaped eggs poured out of its abdomen. At first repulsed, she grew intrigued inspecting them, then her boss burst in and started screaming. He threatened to fire Diana and Maria both if she didn't start working faster. Her parents, with the grocery back home, would be horrified if they knew that she was a maid; she had told them that she worked downtown as a receptionist.

In the short time she and Hector had been together in Denver—after nearly two years apart—they'd been trying to make a family, but things were difficult. While their nieces slept two strides away, she refused to make love.

Through the window came a fragmented voice. Then a crackle. She strained. Could it have been the wind? Branches scraping the screen?

"Honey, did you hear that?" she whispered and burrowed her hips into Hector's.

A crash shook the house and Maria bolted upright. Wood splintered in the front room. Light beams cascaded off the walls as heavy shapes barged into their room. Next to her, Hector's muscles tightened, then he sprang at the shapes. There came a thud like a glove-clap, a grunt, then a swarming in the middle of the room. Screams pierced the air. The overhead light snapped on, and in that first searing glimpse, the room teemed with enormous black insects staring at her with goggled eyes. She pulled the sheet over her thin shorts and tank top. One of the insects thrust the mouth of a machine gun in her face.

¡Mierda! she thought. Hector lay motionless on the floor. What would happen now? She should've never come to Denver.

"Stop screaming, ma'am, and for the last time, put your hands on top of your head," one of them said. The insects were police men. Someone had turned her in. Probably that chain-smoking crone at work.

They handcuffed her arms behind her back and cinched the ratchets too tight. Then they pushed her onto the living room floor next to Diana, who was cursing the men and at the same time begging them not to touch her children. They brought the girls, who lassoed their arms around their mother's neck.

To Maria this seemed excessive, all these men with machine guns and clomping boots, looking like they were ready for war, not the arrest and deportation of a twenty-year-old woman. Her thoughts refused to clear. Her hands went numb. Where the front door had been there was only a black rectangle through which came a gust. She turned her face to it, felt its cool fingers on her cheeks. Then came the men in medical scrubs who tiptoed through the house and shooed others away. They carried scientific instruments and began to cluster around Maria and ask her questions: what had she swallowed? what she was planning? She couldn't answer their strange questions because she had no idea what they were talking about. Then they walked her to a windowless van and drove her away.

❖ ❖ ❖

At Anschutz Hospital they led Maria to a room crawling with workers. In the van they gave her a shot that had started her scalp bristling with sweat. A burly man approached and introduced himself as Dr. Klaus Jorde. He seemed three times her size, with enormous hands that closed around hers like a polar bear's paws, yet his voice was lilting and smooth. She felt powerless gazing at his perfect teeth, bronze moustache, and blonde, almost white, hair. His irises looked like two flecks of ice. He leaned over and his broad shoulders blocked the light. Maria had to stop herself from straining forward to seal her lips to his cool eyelids. She understood that such an odd thought could only spring from the medicine, but she allowed the desire to remain.

Dr. Jorde was the first person to hear it directly when he put a stethoscope to her chest and cried out in pain. Half the men in the room drew pistols and aimed them at Maria.

"For Christ's sake, lower your guns," Dr. Jorde said. "That was my fault."

Dr. Jorde determined that the tremors weren't coming from Maria herself, but from the heart of the four-week-old embryo she was carrying. She couldn't feel the unusual heartbeat, a phenomenon that none of the doctors could explain. The physicists theorized that it was because the sound was of such a low frequency and so powerful that it created a buffer zone around its source. Like tsunami waves on the ocean, they said: out on the open water where they form they're harmless swells, but catch them farther away where they crest and they're million-ton engines of destruction. The medical team affirmed that there was a cardiac abnormality, but the mysterious intensity of the heart continued to puzzle everyone.

Maria pleaded for them to stop the tests and to bring Hector, but they ignored her—all except Dr. Jorde, who argued with the others. He insisted that there was no immediate danger and that it would help to have the husband nearby. When they acquiesced, he flashed her a smile, and she took him as her ally.

❖ ❖ ❖

By the time headlines ran the next morning—*Mother of Miracle Embryo Held for Tests, Tiny Heart Trips Seismographs*, etc.—Hector had hired a lawyer, who was demanding to know on what charge they intended to hold Maria. The next day she was allowed to return to her in-laws' house, which was now guarded by the Denver Police. Media workers clogged the street. Using sensitive audio equipment, they claimed to detect the heartbeat. Listen, they said, holding out a headset, amazement scorched on their faces. Can you hear it?

At the zoo a spotted snow leopard expired from stress. Both slow lorises were found dead. The bison trampled each other. The wolf pack turned on itself. Other animals escaped, including the seven-foot Burmese python that somehow squeezed through a parturition in the feeding door. The hippos knocked one of the attendants against a wall and into critical condition. Zoo officials and pet owners across the city complained and exhorted. Look at what she's doing to the animals, they said. Take this woman away. Deport her back to Mexico.

Pro-life groups opposed Maria's deportation and seized upon the opportunity. See, they said, this is undeniable proof of the force of life within every unborn child. Even very early in a pregnancy the heart's beating. This is the voice of God, they said, asserting His anger at this ungodly nation through the most appropriate of all things, a fetus. They funded a popular marketing campaign, and within days cars across the country were papered with *Can You Hear It?* bumper stickers.

This must be the Messiah, some zealous Christians said. Look at the evidence. The mother's name is Maria. Who cares if the father's named Hector? Witness this as proof: in addition to Anschutz, Dr. Jorde also works downtown at St. Joseph's, where the baby will be born. Joseph and Mary, they said. Surely it's the Second Coming.

Hesitant skeptics disbelieved the reports. These people were from every walk of life: plumbers, teachers, priests, bankers, daycare providers, janitors, urban planners, truck drivers. They read every heartbeat article several times to find the gimmick, the flaw in the story that would prove it a joke. They looked at the date it was written, trying to find some significance beyond the claimed reality. They were sure that the whole thing would be exposed as a hoax.

❖ ❖ ❖

What upset Hector most were all the men constantly congregating around Maria; he couldn't get a single moment alone with his wife. Outside, the lights from the camera crews turned night into day and made sleep impossible. He'd lie awake and stare at a rectangle of artificial light on the wall, fearing how this would end. All he wanted was a big family and a ranch where he could raise champion fighting roosters. His cousin in Aguascalientes promised to provide a line of pure-bred Louisiana reds—and from those he would start his business.

A reporter banged on the window. Hector charged onto the porch. A few of the bastards glanced his way, but the camera's bright light disarmed him. He rubbed his side, where the police had cracked two ribs during the house attack. Hector was a stout young man with a thin moustache and tight-furrowed brow. His high-school nickname was Perro de Toro after the breed of bulldog he bred. He wore a white button-down shirt, black jeans, and a turquoise-studded belt buckle that had been his only personal indulgence for a long time. During the past two years he built a life around saving for Maria. When she finally arrived she wasn't the carefree girl he remembered, but he stuck to his routine, working six days a week for as many hours as possible. On his day off there were labor jobs for five bucks an hour, sometimes less. He told the reporter that he was happy that his wife was pregnant, that they had been hoping for a child, that he was glad his son or daughter had such a strong heart.

The reporters clamored to meet the mother-to-be. Five days after Olympia's warning, a single reporter was allowed into the house.

No, she didn't think it was divine conception. She and Hector had made love a few weeks ago on a Tuesday afternoon when he came home early from work because of a hailstorm. No one else had been home. Yes, Maria was a practicing Catholic, just like she'd been raised. There'd been no divine visions or voices that she could recall. The afternoon lovemaking wasn't out of the ordinary other than that they didn't make love as often as either of them might like, therefore it'd been especially nice. Plus, the sound of the rain was romantic. Maria paused and blushed. She was a petite girl with long black hair and a crescent scar under her left eye from a bike wreck when she was nine. Her eyes stung a little; she'd been raised not to discuss such things.

The reporter persisted.

No, neither of them had been drinking. She didn't smoke, either. Of course no drugs. They made love on their bed as the window rattled in its frame, then she got up and cooked dinner. She couldn't remember what, probably something simple since she wasn't as good of a cook as her mother. Tacos or spaghetti or burgers. She felt nothing unpleasant other than some recent nausea. No, she didn't have maternity benefits, are you kidding? Yes, she'd seen a sonogram of the embryo; it looked like a tiny backwards six. She *was* very sorry for the animals at the zoo and for those people who'd lost pets, but what could she do?

❖ ❖ ❖

Each morning people tuned in to see whether the heart was still beating. It didn't disappoint. Twice per second it drummed out its rhythm. The media workers unplugged their headsets but kept them as dampers over their ears as they stared, benumbed, into twitching cups of coffee. Over time, the heartbeat's intensity increased. It hammered away, deepening

and speeding, until each beat struck with the force
of a small explosion. In nearby houses, mirrors and
windows cracked, screens loosened and swung free,
dishes shivered toward counter edges, books tumbled
from shelves, doors rejected their jambs. Neighbors who could left town. Those who stayed wore
twenty-dollar ear filters or took sleeping pills or drank
themselves into stupor.

Always there remained around Maria the buffer
zone, which increased in size with the heartbeat's
growing intensity. At first it encompassed a room.
By the second week it extended to the house itself,
and by the third it spread outside. The police officers
crowded into this sanctuary. They shook their heads
and clenched their jaws. One of them snorkled and
spat into the yard. They watched the gob of phlegm
shiver. Like the eye of a goddamn hurricane, the one
in charge said.

"*Es un milagro*," her mother said when Maria called.
Her parents hadn't wanted her to go to the U.S.,
hadn't really wanted her to marry Hector, because,
they argued, their families were too different. But
this changed everything. It was proof of divine affir-
mation. "Every hour I've been praying to the Virgin
for you."

Maria knew that her mother meant the icon
hanging over the desk in the small office of her
parents' bodega. It was a painting of Mary done by
an amateur artist and obscured by a haze of age. It
had been in their family for generations. Maria used
to imagine that under the grime, Mary's robe was

a vibrant blue, electric even, and that her downcast
invisible eyes matched its color. But now the painting
struck Maria, in her memory of it, as lifeless. She cut
short the conversation.

There was a part of Maria that wanted to use her
mother's faith to interpret her troubles. She should
humble herself and accept her fate. What was it that
Mary said when the angel appeared? *I am the Lord's
servant, may it be to me as you have said.* But the Virgin
Mother didn't have doctors scanning her abdomen
every fifteen minutes, government men hovering, cell
phones ringing, a satellite feed to the White House.
And this crazy heartbeat.

It seemed more likely that this was punishment
for something—disobeying her parents, despising
coworkers, not loving Hector enough. Was it letting
the coyote do what he did? She hadn't told Hector,
but she was the first to arrive at that restaurant on
the Aguascalientes outskirts. The coyote was a small
man with a clean-shaven face and cat-like eyes. She
couldn't decide his age, somewhere between 40 and
60. He hurried her into the back of his delivery truck,
followed her in, and closed the door. Sweat broke
from her pores. There was no ventilation, and even
though it was seven in the morning the truck was
sweltering. He hinted that he wanted to kiss her, that
he wouldn't drive her until she let him. She didn't kiss
back, but when he put his hand inside her blouse, she
pushed him away. She struggled, but he wrestled her
to the truck bed then slapped her hard across the face.
The wheel well dug into her back. He opened her

shirt and had taken out his sex, was about to press it to her lips, when a whisper came at the door. Then a knock. He flashed a look of warning at her, and she would've screamed if he hadn't tucked himself in and opened the door. It was a man with his wife and baby.

Then so much happened during the crossing itself. She had nearly died, crammed into the truck's spare gas tank. When Hector came to pick her up, she collapsed into his arms and couldn't speak for days. By the time her voice returned it didn't seem right to mention the incident. She knew that it would change the way he thought about her. Plus, he was so happy that they were finally together. So she kept quiet, intending to bring it up when the time was right.

A distance grew between them over the summer. They hadn't even watched a single sunset together. After all, Hector was the one, through friends, who had arranged for the coyote and told her where to meet him. In her husband she saw, with her mother's insight, a hasty young man. She tried repenting of such thoughts. When she could she retreated to the bedroom, and before even kneeling, the Hail Mary flowed past her lips like a fast-running spring, a release that only subsided with a knock at the door.

Dr. Jorde visited twice a day for at least an hour, each time his arrival marked by an unmistakable creaking of the porch steps. His questions, put forth in that smooth voice, made her want to talk, until she was telling him about her childhood and youth: about playing in the grocery storeroom with her friends, about seeing how long she could tolerate the walk-in freezer—always longer than anyone—and about sneaking out at night. She responded with questions of her own, and he told her about growing up in Norway, fishing with his father on a tiny boat and slipping away to the forest to read adventure books. Dr. Jorde was so large and his hair so frosty white that she caught herself comparing him to her father, who was so different—small and dark—but who exuded a similar sense of masculine calm.

At twelve weeks, the government decided to fly Maria and Hector to a military clinic on the Yuma Proving Grounds in thinly populated southwestern Arizona. It's an alien baby, bloggers said when they heard. Otherwise why take her to a top-secret military base? She was abducted and impregnated. Just wait and see. They'll claim she had a miscarriage and we'll never hear another word.

What the hell, the Indians on the Fort Yuma Indian Reservation said. Why bring her here? We don't want her or her loud baby. Can't you leave us alone out here in the middle of nowhere where you put us in the first place?

The hesitant skeptics watched developments with somber intensity. When they heard talk show hosts and coworkers joking about the heartbeat, they no longer laughed. They woke early and, before brewing coffee, opened the paper or went online. They grew pensive, unable to shake the feeling that something terrible had come upon the world and that they were cursed or at least deeply unlucky for having lived during the generation of its arrival.

❖ ❖ ❖

At the Yuma clinic they put Maria in a sterile white room and badgered her with tests. Rashes bloomed on her skin from the adhesive electrodes. They peered into her eyes and ears, stabbed her with needles, touched cold metal to her privates. One day, without her asking, they told her that the fetus's sex was male.

"I want Dr. Jorde," Maria said. The scar under her left eye glowed pink.

"He's not available, he's just a regular doctor," the government man said.

Maria wrenched the electrodes from her chest. "No more tests until you get him." She flushed at her own anger. Hector grabbed the man by the collar and brandished a fist in his face. He scurried away.

The next day, Dr. Jorde lumbered into the room, his light hair shimmering, his chest as wide as a refrigerator.

"Please don't let them do anymore tests," she said.

"You're going to be fine, you and your baby. I'll be with you from now on." He squeezed her hand, and for the first time in weeks she relaxed.

❖ ❖ ❖

Hector sat in the lounge, sipping reconstituted soup. He was replaying in his mind a recent discussion with Dr. Jorde. "I strongly advise against intercourse," the man had said. "We don't know how it might affect the fetus, so it's risky. Have you two had any sexual relations since you've been here at Yuma?"

The way the doctor drew out certain words, *riiisky* and *sehhksual*—as if he talked in sing-song to avoid stuttering—annoyed Hector. He knew Maria liked this doctor, and he *was* the only person besides Maria who spoke to him here, but some of his *questions*.

"Are you kidding?" Hector had said. "She can't even take a crap without you people watching."

"That's probably *behhhst* then," the doctor said and left.

Hector decided to carry his soup down the hall to check on Maria. The room in which they insisted she spend most of her time had a window that overlooked a field of yellow scrub grass. The scientists claimed that the heartbeat's radius had grown to more than a mile—and the buffer zone's to the length of four city blocks. He tried to picture these two concentric ripples chasing each other. How could something invisible overwhelm their lives like this?

He leaned against the doorframe and watched Maria as she read by the window. She was so edgy lately. Silent and moody. Darker, older. He kept expecting her to snap out of it. They were still young; they could make something of their lives when this was all over.

"What're you reading?" he asked.

"Nothing," she said. "Why, do you really want to know?"

"That's okay, I'm just killing time, waiting for my soup to cool." He passed a hand over its escaping steam. He couldn't tell whether she wanted to talk. "It's so boring here."

"At least you're not getting a new test every five minutes," she snapped. There was that note in her voice with its accusatory edge. What had he done?

"If they're bothering you so much, why don't you talk to your doctor friend about it?" he said. When she slammed the magazine onto the nightstand, he felt the excitement of confrontation like a fuse lighting inside him.

"Why don't you like him? Because he's so smart?"

"He's creepy. Just now he asked me whether we've been having sex."

"You're just jealous."

Hector winced and felt the excitement fizzle out. He needed to feel this heartbeat for himself. He set his soup on the nightstand and said, "I'm going for a walk."

❖ ❖ ❖

After the clinic's air conditioning, the desert wind felt good. Though it was twilight, wavy heat lines lingered above the grass. Hector headed for the golf course.

Halfway down the first fairway, just past the point where the trees became leafless, it felt like a mattress hit him from behind. His legs gave way and he was thrown to his hands and knees. By the time he had recovered and started to stand up, another burst crashed into him so hard that he felt his rib bones strain against their vertebral attachments. His knee and shoulder joints flexed and ground together. Between bursts came a liquid gurgle, which filled the air like a cataract. A fear that he hadn't known since childhood, pure and powerful, rushed over him. One day when he was ten years old, he stood on a canyon rim and gazed down at the Mezquital River. The whitewater resembled a snaking path of concrete at the base of the granite walls. Directly below, just past the lip over which he curled his toes, lay a pool of black—and in it his family, who shouted and waved and called for him to jump. His legs chattered. He closed his eyes and imagined the worst, his body scraping against the cliff and ending in a crushed and bloody mess. That's all it took. He accepted that possibility, then he stepped off.

That was courage: the ability to act against your own wellbeing. It also came with a thrill that maddened the pulse. He got to his feet and walked farther, bracing himself against the heartbeats. Perched atop a tee-box, he gazed west, out over the prairie, out over America. The sinking sun painted the clouds purple, and he imagined being back in Denver, taking his son to football games and playing catch in the yard, the boy growing older and stronger. With each resounding beat, these visions sharpened and grew more possible even as they nearly knocked him again to his knees. He saw many years into the future, his girls and boys playing together on the family ranch. Then disorientation struck. The sky and grass wheeled. He turned, intending to run, but his body's circuits refused to connect. He pitched headfirst into the rough on the eighteenth hole.

When the buffer zone expanded far enough so that it was safe, they retrieved Hector's corpse.

Experts explained that percussive bursts of audio energy vibrate the inner ear and can rupture internal organs. At such levels and for a prolonged period, the heartbeat was, as everyone saw, deadly. Maria was inconsolable. Dr. Jorde ordered sedatives but was cautious not to harm the fetus.

❖❖❖

The tiny airports in the nearby towns overflowed with incoming flights as the religious and the curious and the suspicious from around the world flew in to get close enough to experience the heartbeat. They aimed rental cars down highways lined with sagebrush, then, driving into the expanding sound waves, they said to each other, There, that was it just then, did you feel it?

A group of devotees formed on the western edge of the proving grounds, camping out, waiting, thrilled when the heartbeat finally expanded to envelop them. They wanted to be the vanguard, so they followed its leading edge. All day they hiked away from Maria, carrying backpacks and water. Toward nightfall, when they were far enough away that it had grown faint, they pitched tents. When it woke them in early morning with its pounding, they broke camp and began hiking again. Each day the radius swelled at a faster rate, until this group had to be rescued by helicopters. Three holdouts refused to board, and, as happened with Hector, they perished.

Two days before it reached Yuma, a man shot his entire family then turned the gun on himself. Apocalyptic murders echoed across the country. A handful of Yuma residents refused to leave, gathering instead at a local bar. One of them telephoned a major news station, which broadcast the group's death throes.

The hesitant skeptics bore silent witness. By now they hardly slept and took whole days off from work to research theories and make plans. They noted with increased concern the new bumper stickers appearing: *Pro-choice (I told you so)*; *I don't care if you are Catholic—God wants that heart stopped*; *Can You Abort It?*

❖ ❖ ❖

On Christmas Eve, Maria, Dr. Jorde, and the thirty government employees safe but now trapped within the buffer zone, boarded a KC-135. It took off and crawled upward in a tight spiral to avoid population centers. Maria trembled in one of the seats. She dug fingernails into her fists and tried not to think about the airplane's enclosed space. Or about Hector. She tried instead to picture her parents, to count the wrinkles around her father's eyes, like cracked clay, and her mother's cheeks, plump as tomatoes. The plane jostled and her stomach lurched. She was a widow at twenty. Why was this happening to her? That she'd been short with Hector the last time they spoke—not to mention that she'd caused him to take that deadly walk—haunted her. She could hardly think about him without her insides tangling. And now they were flying her to some Antarctic outpost. She felt the baby's first swirl then leaned forward and vomited.

To ease her claustrophobia Dr. Jorde secured a spot for her in the cockpit. From there she gazed at

the endless blue sky, marveling at its cloudlessness.
The decision to move her to the Carivelli Research
Station on the Sabrina Coast, located at 67° S 113° E,
sparked international furor. The move put countries
with coasts on the Southern and Indian Oceans at
great peril. Together with Australia and New Zealand,
nations in Asia and Africa sent their entire air forces
against the KC-135. American jets intercepted the
attackers and downed several dozen planes, but there
were too many. Listening on a headset, Maria heard
the American pilots' final transmissions.

"I've got the mark. One mark—" Static.

"He's at six angels. Goddam—" Static.

"Fox one! Fox one!—" Static.

The American jets, it turned out, needn't have
bothered. Missile range was only six miles, and long
before reaching that point, the attacking jets broke
up from the massive sound waves. The KC-135 pilot
pointed at a spot on the horizon where they could
see the death of the jets in dreamlike flashes of white
on the ocean's dark face.

❖ ❖ ❖

At Carivelli, Maria continued her silence. It wasn't
that she chose not to speak, simply that her voice
was unpredictable. When she thought about saying
something, the muscles in her throat fluttered with
such frightening force that she couldn't trust them.

Some days she donned boots, a parka, gloves, and
goggles then walked out onto the tundra. Dr. Jorde
often came along. She thought that he wanted to

keep an eye on her, that he might suspect her of planning to throw herself into the freezing water by the shore, but she was always glad when he joined. Sometimes he talked—about the rocky soil far underfoot or the gossip among the technicians who had accompanied them or news from back home. One day he told her about the way that the ground on which they walked was made up of snowmelt, the thinnest layers of snow thawing from ground heat and then freezing, a gradual accrual that allowed them, essentially, to walk on water. Maria found comfort in the thought, that all around them were extraordinary phenomena. Mostly, though, they walked without speaking, and she listened to his deep breaths and the frozen ground crunching underfoot.

She tried to see herself as Dr. Jorde must, a simple girl who'd married too young and had somehow brought a terrible curse upon the world. He never questioned her silence but didn't stop asking questions, which she answered with a nod or head shake. One afternoon as they paused atop a ridge, she caught herself gazing into the reflective lenses of Dr. Jorde's goggles, imagining those cool specks underneath, and she knew her voice had returned.

"I keep hoping to see a polar bear," she said.

He chuckled, and she could tell that he took her speaking as a good sign.

"I hate to be the one to break it to you," he said from under his moustache, which was combed with frost, "but polar bears only live in the Arctic. In fact, there aren't many mammals down here at all. If you

keep your eyes on the shore, though, you might spot
a seal, maybe a penguin."

The cold bored into her cheeks. She wanted to
reach out to him, touch him. She had no one here.
She thought of spooning with Hector.

"How far out are they?" she asked.

"About two hundred miles."

Maria pictured what that meant, waves of destruction being sent out from her womb. Was it intentional?
Perhaps by keeping it she was willing it, too.

"I don't want to hurt anyone else," she said.

"Of course you don't," Dr. Jorde said. He placed
a gloved hand on her shoulder. "I understand. You
know I'm here, whatever you decide."

Reflected in his goggles were two endless expanses
of white. She scanned the landscapes-in-miniature
for signs of life but saw nothing.

❖ ❖ ❖

When the heartbeat hit Melbourne, the blasts moved
in quarter-mile increments, desiccating glass and
pulverizing concrete, so that spouts of misted material
rose into the air as if from the footsteps of an invisible giant marching north. Bolts loosened, I-beams
buckled, buildings pancaked. Within hours the city
was reduced to rubble and the rubble reduced to sand.

That same day, India launched a cruise missile
at Carivelli. It shattered in the air and dropped its
warhead into the Southern Ocean. The Australian
deaths outraged even the hesitant skeptics. They
renounced their silence, chastised themselves for not

acting sooner, and marched in the streets shoulder-to-shoulder with the bloggers, the conspiracy theorists, the zealous Christians, the pro-lifers and pro-choicers and expecting mothers—all of them demanding that the fetal heart be stopped. Someone should've killed that girl in Denver when we still had a chance, they said to each other, full of righteous indignation.

"What's the worth of my baby's life if it costs thousands of others?" Maria asked.

Dr. Jorde said that her situation was terrible, but he couldn't tell her what to do. "The world's never seen anything like this baby's heart," he said. "Who knows? Maybe there's a reason for all the suffering. Maybe we'll only understand after it's born. Maybe not even then."

Via satellite phone she called her parents. Her mother's voice came to her like bolts rattling inside an empty can. "*Maria, estás embarazada con el anticristo.*"

It seemed impossible that her mother could say such a thing. "But you said it was a miracle," Maria protested. "Why would God give me a baby and expect me not to have it?"

How could she justify ending its life, her only remaining connection with Hector? She felt sorry for the others, especially those who'd died, but she hadn't intended for its heart to be so strong. If it wasn't supposed to be born, then why was there this strange buffer zone around her, protecting her and making it so that she felt nothing? If there was anyone to blame, it wasn't her, it was God.

"I'm going to have it," she told her mother and closed the connection. She looked at Dr. Jorde and saw the faintest upturn in the corner of his mouth.

"Fine, Maria. That's just fine." He held his arms open, and she buried her face in the downy pillows of his jacket.

❖ ❖ ❖

Maria stepped onto the submersible's traction-gridded ladder. She gripped the tiny hatch's edge and lowered herself through the opening. Inside, it was like a closet. As they descended, the porthole went from emerald to black. More than ever, she wanted her mother.

The console blanketed them in a blue light. Whiskers shaded Dr. Jorde's face. At Carivelli, he'd shed weight, seemed to have shrunk in every direction. His eyes no longer radiated but looked small and dark. His hair had been cropped, leaving only stubble. How well did she really know him? He wasn't a father himself, didn't even have a family, he had said. Something heavy settled onto her chest and her vision grew dim. It felt like she was once again crumpled into a ball, her insides jolting, her lung muscles clutching for air, her ears splitting from the thunder in this tank where the coyote had shoved her, anger flashing in his eyes. Now he's killing her, eliminating evidence. Engine heat pours in. As she shifts, the shank of a bolt digs into her knee and releases a stream of blood that runs down her shin into her tennis shoe. The odor of gasoline burns her throat. She bangs the walls with her fists, claws into them with her nails, but the roar and jostle and heat persist as they drive along some highway toward some fiancé in some American city. While Maria cashiered at the bodega, saving money and writing letters to Hector, the idea of working to escape her life and start afresh had been enough to sustain her. With gasoline fumes gnawing at her lungs, she feels the full weight of her naiveté. What's real is that she's one of the unlucky ones who die crammed into small spaces, their end hellish and confusing.

Then a gasp of air and sunlight on her face, the rough texture of asphalt against her back, a breeze tickling her arm hair. It's as if she's been elsewhere for years. She gulps fresh air as the coyote tugs her standing and shoves a cell phone into her hand.

She made it then, but that ride only lasted half of a day. She would be in this submersible with these two men for weeks. The tiny porthole stared, black and unblinking. Just as she started to scream, cool fingers interlaced with hers.

"Everything's going to be all right," Dr. Jorde said in his liquid voice. "We'll get through this together."

Maria gripped his hand, her only lifeline as they sank deeper.

❖ ❖ ❖

The waters above the Marianas Trench floated with the corpses of whales, sharks, dolphins, fish, manatees, squids, and the husks of anemones, desmid, plankton, and rockweed that had been shocked to death and dislodged. Coral fragments studded the mix. The carcasses, bloated by depressurization, burst open and released great clouds of decay. The ruined marine life rode the edges of monster waves driven forward by the sonic blasts.

The group was able to survive for three weeks in the ocean's aphotic zone. The pilot gave her duties: monitor gauges for hull pressure and watch a radar screen for possible obstructions. She almost made it into the eighth month. With a portable ultrasound machine Dr. Jorde produced a sonogram. He pointed to the heart.

"Looks perfectly normal," he said. "About the size of an apricot, slightly bigger." He gave her the specially-adapted stethoscope then clicked on a small lamp and held the sonogram under its beam. Had Maria not been watching closely, she would've missed it, the slightest shake of his head in what she could only interpret as wonder.

❖ ❖ ❖

In the third trimester, on the nineteenth day of the first month, in the twenty-third year of the third millennium, two hundred thirty-one days since Olympia's announcement, after tsunamis wracked numerous coastlines, whole cities vanished in deluge, nations went to war, and governments collapsed, Dr. Jorde began the preparations to attempt a cesarean section. He'd brought the necessary tools and the pilot assisted.

"I'm going to put you to sleep," Dr. Jorde said. "It'll be easiest."

Maria imagined the relief of never waking up. But what would the world without her be like? She couldn't know, only that even if she died, her baby, with its strong heart, would survive to old age.

"Can I hear it one last time?" she asked.

"Why don't you listen to it while you fall asleep," Dr. Jorde said.

He put the special stethoscope in her ears and placed the mask over her nose and mouth. His pulse thrummed in his fingertips as they brushed her cheek. A bead of sweat thickened at his temple and glimmered blue as it rolled across his forehead. The heartbeat plunked away until, like hoof beats fading into the distance, it decreased. Maria sensed, then, that something like a pressurized column of air had been holding her aloft for the past few months and understood that she was finally being lowered, gently, from what all along was a great and terrifying height.

❖

THE WRETCH

The crowd parts for a ragamuffin. It's a boy who has stopped in their flow like a rock in a river. He stands and tilts his head and gazes up at the clock's eye that floats in the air above the rail station. Down the street Old Trinity tolls the hour. Its waves roll out over the churchyard tombstones and incite a delirious murmuring. Then a figure in sackcloth and rags steps out from the crowd. From within a corkscrew of fingernails, she offers the boy a tin horn.

The boy catches her odor, mold and stale excrement, and pulls back. But the tin horn gleams. "How much is it?"

The woman buried inside the rag pile cackles. She thrusts the horn into his hands. Disappears. Old Trinity's waves canyon down streets and fetch past a man with a Christmas tree over his shoulder, past a woman staggering under an armful of string-tied packages, and past a pair of rubbish pickers squabbling over a bone.

The boy hugs the prize.

❖ ❖ ❖

A mangled roar. Hawkers shouting, hooves clopping, car bells jingling, rifles cracking. And the quince of the city: spent gunpowder, horse dung, evergreen. Inside a rollicking oyster-house, a dozen girls sit in the laps of gentlemen as waiters carry foaming glasses of beer stacked pyramidally on trays. Outside, highbinders and rowdies squat on cheese boxes and watch for an easy mark. A gaggle of youths blowing penny whistles sweeps under the wet skins of hundreds of turkeys impaled on hooks and shining in lamplight. The streets teem with men and women in fancy clothes. The boy slips a hand into his pocket and runs a fingertip along the horn.

He finds the place, a shop with a lighted window display of red, green, and blue dresses and brightly colored material. He's been here before.

❖ ❖ ❖

"Again no receipt!" Alarms go off in the boy's head when the Madam clots him on the ear. She snatches the ribbons from his fist, clamps his face with a doughy palm. "What took you so long, wretch?"

His gaze drifts and settles on the new girl, Mathilde, the one with eyes the color of holly leaves. She sits in the window seat and takes it all in.

"There was an old woman—"

"And?"

The horn grows so large that it strains his pocket stitches. "She crossed me."

157

"Crossed you, you say. And what did she want, hmm?"

The horn's bell bites his ribs. "She wouldn't say."

Purple veins hatch the Madam's cheeks. "I should give you to the Russian this instant."

❖ ❖ ❖

Inside the upstairs closet, the boy peels back wallpaper and pulls out a timepiece and a silk necktie from a cranny. Buries his face in the resplendent red and black stripes, inhales the spicy scent of his father's neck, imagines its whiskery roughness and the soft glide of his mother's fingertips on his back. The timepiece's arms hold their frozen shrug. "These hands mark the minute of their passing," a fireman said, and the thought conjures an image: a can with a curved spout at the end of a small boy's arm (his arm?) and, pouring from the spout, a gold ribbon of oil about to strike the coals below.

The horn glints with the old woman's grease. Her moldy richness ripens the closet air. He presses the mouthpiece to his lips, tastes the metal tang. The old woman is a witch with magnificent powers, but if he sounds the horn, he becomes her slave.

How does he know this? He just does.

❖ ❖ ❖

Angel and the boy watch the lacy flame on a candle. Grunts and gasps come from the next room, Mathilde with her first mark. Angel cradles the boy's head against her chest. She wears a red silk choker. Her eyes are black buttons, her eyebrows a pair of dark caterpillars. When one of Mathilde's cries escapes, Angel strokes the boy's hair. They wait like that for a long time.

The boy wakes to Angel squeezing his shoulder. "Now," she whispers and blows out the candle. He listens as she slides back the wall panel that gives access to the next room. The boy passes through on tiptoe into a cave that stinks of sweat and gin. He makes his fingertips as soft as cotton. Passes them along a dresser top.

"Over here," Mathilde whispers. "In his coat."

He reaches toward her voice, arms outstretched. She touches his shoulder as she slips past. The man stirs. From a coat draped over a chair, the boy extracts a pocketbook. He pulls out a thin chain at the end of which dangles the weight of something heavy, something that will please the Madam. But it catches an edge, then swings free and clanks against the bed frame. The boy turns to run but it's too late. His jacket bunches under his arms as he's hoisted into the air to become a punching bag on a string.

✧ ✧ ✧

A blue glow coats the city. The Madam drags him by the arm past piles of bricks and rows of iron girders and coils of steel cables. He grits his teeth against the pain in his sides, which are stained black with bruises. Near the water she heaves her bulk against a wooden gate that shrieks open. Then they climb a ramp into fog. They go up and up as sewer gas and river smells fill the air. Somewhere far below, a steamer whistle blows. The Madam chuffs and snarls as she tugs him along.

"Where are we going?"

She woofs through her lips, stops and roughly strokes his head. "Be still, please. I'm taking you to see something."

They walk farther, then she turns and steps up on the curb. Overhead, a cable as thick as a man's waist loops down out of the fog. She peers over the balustrade. "Take a good look," she says and beckons him up.

He stands on tiptoe and strains to look over. She clamps him under the arms and hoists him up onto the balustrade. Below stretches a floor of gray. Her hand spreads across his back.

"You always wanted to see your parents."

The fog receives him before the cry in his throat can escape.

❖ ❖ ❖

Dark lines web the sky. He's on his back, gliding through the water. Something has him by the wrist. Then he feels rocks knuckling under him. A sour finger probes his mouth. He tastes decay and death. Finds his hands and knees and lets watery strings unspool from between his lips onto the rocks. When he's able, he gets to his feet—and there the witch stands in all her ragged glory, lamped by the purple glow of the sky.

She pulls something from within her sackcloth that catches the light. A blade that flashes silver.

She moves toward him, holds out the handle. "Now, clock boy, take up your work."

He runs.

❖ ❖ ❖

Races up the stairs. Throws open the closet. Tears back the wallpaper. All his treasures—gone.

❖ ❖ ❖

Then the Russian. On a cold afternoon, the boy sits on cotton ticking inside a third-floor room with a knobless door. Somehow a bluebottle fly has made its way in. He watches it crawl up and down the window as he shivers from the cold. Outside on the stoop, the Madam talks with a man as tall as a lamp-post. He's wrapped in a sheepskin coat cinched at the waist with a rope. Black fur hat. Thick red beard. She points toward the window and the giant looks up. A smile twists inside his beard. The boy forgets that he's a boy.

❖ ❖ ❖

In the parlor the Russian gazes out the window, his back so broad that it blocks the light. The Madam cajoles, offers tea and rum, places a hand on the giant's elbow then starts when he pulls it away. Since the boy's return from the river, she won't look at him. He stands in the doorway beside Angel. The Madam says, "The child is getting too big, I can't keep him. But he would be very useful to you. And Angel, of course, is yours for the night."

The giant grunts, says, "I'm Red Koko."

"The wretch of the bowery," Angel whispers in the boy's ear.

Red Koko turns toward them, bent so that his head won't brush the ceiling. He sidesteps the chandelier. His sideburns twine into the fur of his hat. His eyebrows meet in a solid mass, his moustache upcurls at both ends over swollen lips. He stabs the air with a finger.

The boy's bones turn to jelly, his muscles to water.

"Look at you," Red Koko says. "You're not a boy. You're a *kukla*."

❖❖❖

Kept in Red Koko's cellar, the boy grows weak. He squats over a grate and releases a runny essence that saps his strength. Vinegary sweat clings to his skin. During the day he repairs the glass plates that are stacked neatly in long rows along the walls. He polishes out pits and rubs them with special rags, tacks the edges flat with a small hammer.

There are two rooms here, his favorite the one with the stone-mullioned squares of light near the ceiling. If he climbs atop stacked crates and places an ear to the squares, city sounds come through: wheels clattering over cobblestones, a bottle shattering, a woman calling another a cunt, the cry of an injured cat.

The boy holds the glass plates to the light, watches the dark hatchings resolve into a young woman wearing only undergarments. She's solid and transparent at once, and she looks softly at him. Sometimes a glass plate contains the inverted world, and he'll hold it up for as long as his arms can stand, studying the girl's skin gone dark, her glowing eyes, the couch or bed a ghosted wash of white like a fish's underbelly.

With each plate he touches, he summons the witch's power by leaving a mark—breath mist, fingernail nick, palm sweat—before running to squat over the grate and emptying himself.

❖ ❖ ❖

Red Koko throws open the cellar door. He stands in a rectangle of sun so bright that the boy can hardly look. The giant wears tall leather boots buffed to a crimson gleam. A whiff of something sweet floats in on the air. "Time to go to work, my little *kukolka*." He stuffs tobacco into a pipe and lights it. Plumes of smoke billow out. "Even spring carries no joy in this country."

❖ ❖ ❖

A stench hits the boy when he enters the room. It's dark. His jaw stings. He coughs and sneezes.

"Breathe through your mouth," Red Koko says. He attaches a match flame to a candle inside a box made of red glass that causes a bloody patina to coat everything. Here there are old plates stained with age that hold the shriveled faces of people with proud looks: women in high-collared dresses. Men with gloves, canes, sabers. Children, too, blurred like doves' wings.

Red Koko sets a plate with a man and woman atop a blank one. He withdraws the window shroud and sets them in a streak of sunlight.

"*Raz, dva, tri, chiteri,*" he says, then lets the shroud flip shut. He slides the plate into a bath and upturns a waist-pinched vial. Like smoke condensing into solid, the inverted faces appear, somehow snared by the glass.

"Magic," the boy says.

"*Nyet.* Ancestors for the rich. Only beggars no longer come from Dutch."

❖ ❖ ❖

The ancestors refuse to appear for the boy. The sun-winked plates turn to shadow in the baths. When Red Koko's out one day, the boy submerges a finished plate in a chemical tray. The ancestors on it slide from the glass like shed skin. He tries another and another. The baths turn black. Nothing remains but empty glass. He sighs in relief. The witch has begun her work.

To urge her on, he rubs sweat on the trays of bromide and collodion, dribbles piss into the vials of mercury and cyanide, dips his hands into the water buckets. He smears spit on the eye of the black hooded machine in the corner. He thinks *hex, hex, hex.*

He pries open a locked door and discovers a room with plates of young girls. Rows of sand timers. Inside a metal trunk there's a box, and inside the box he finds his father's necktie and timepiece along with the witch's horn. He touches the horn's bore, its pocked bell. Places the mouthpiece against his lips for the second time.

Somewhere the witch is waiting.

❖ ❖ ❖

The boy is put back in the cellar, but one day Red Koko takes him on an errand. He scampers to keep up with the giant, who strides through bowery shadows, past soda fountains, cheap wares, peanut vendors. The giant rains pipe embers onto the shoulders of the those who fail to move away fast enough. A whip made of wires dangles at his waist. "Remember," he says, "a woman is not made of glass."

The Madam is waiting on the stoop. She scowls at the boy but turns to Red Koko. "She's locked herself in her room. Be sure to get my clothes back."

Red Koko stomps open the door. In a flash, he lifts Angel and strips off her dress. Tosses her onto the bed and tears open her petticoats until she's bare-skinned. He unhooks the whip from his belt and, holding her wrists above her head, marks her chest across both breasts with crimson stripes.

The boy lunges for Koko, wraps himself around a tree-trunk thigh.

The giant laughs and lifts Angel by the hair. Her eyes rim white. He licks her cheeks with his bright red tongue, says, "Tears are only water." When she spits at him, he brings the whip across her face.

❖ ❖ ❖

Rainwater floods the cellar. It pulls the captured women and girls from the glass plates in dark threads. The frames rust and crumble away. Then the cellar room is rented to an Italian family who sleep in their clothes on filthy mattresses. Upstairs, spores sprout like evil eyes in the baths. The chemicals exude the stench of rotting flesh. Red Koko stomps the floors, drums the walls with his fists. The images streak, the well water turns orange, the sand timers clog.

Witch work.

❖ ❖ ❖

Late on a rainy night, Red Koko finds the sycamore tree in the park along Water Street. He paces eight strides east and begins slinging mud with a shovel. When he can stand knee-deep in the hole, he buries the box that holds the necktie, the timepiece, and the tin horn. He pats the earth and scans the park and lets the rainwater conceal his work.

❖ ❖ ❖

Red Koko hefts the hooded machine over a shoulder and tells the boy to follow. "Today you'll have your portrait with a family. The rich have their sorrows, too."

Inside the enormous house, which smells like fresh cotton and linseed oil, the boy can hardly take in all the wonderful things. Patterned carpets, lamps, glittering metal, a fireplace. An organ! The mother wears a blue silk dress, her hair a cloud of golden curls. She's the most beautiful woman he's ever seen. Her lips move constantly but her voice is a tiny whisper: "...he's so pale...hasn't got a name?...we'll call him Cyrus...we had a Cyrus..."

The twin daughters, barely old enough to walk, are miniature replicas of their mother. The father wears a red neck scarf. The boy is made to bathe, then the father combs the boy's hair and wedges him into a suit. They stand in a blisteringly bright courtyard, the boy posed next to the girls, who grin and make eyes at him. Red Koko disappears under the black hood, and there's only the glass eye fixed on them.

Lies, the boy thinks. *What this machine tells are lies.*

❖ ❖ ❖

He's sent to spend more time with the family. Upon arrival, he's washed and combed and put into the scratchy suit. They eat supper then catch a car to the park.

They pass under an enormous white arch and the air grows sweet.

"Honeysuckle," the father says as he runs a gloved finger around the rim of his top hat. "Best time of the year, my boy."

The mother takes the boy's hand and they stroll toward drifting voices and oar splashes. They pass gas-lit carvings traced into yellow stone. In one, a tiger rubs its head lovingly against a sheep. In another, a man stands with his arms out as giant insects lift him into the air by his wrists. Somewhere in the city a bell tolls. On the terrace, Hana and Biddy tug at the boy's sleeves, each wanting to be picked up to see over the balustrade.

"Cyrus, pwease, Cyrus, pwease," they say.

The boy lifts Hana and holds her under the arms
as they all watch the red and blue candles of pleasure
boaters drifting in the dark.

Strains of music draw them toward a plaza ringed
with fine-wired bird cages atop iron posts. The mother
murmurs the names of the flowers—"...wisteria...
roses...baby's breath..."—while the father taps
statues with his cane and says, "Brownstone, granite,
bronze." They eat ice cream and drink mineral water
under a pavilion. They ride hobby horses. Hana and
Biddy cling to the boy.

That night he's put to bed on a feather mattress,
but he can't sleep for the recurring dream of holding
the girls atop the terrace balustrade. Somehow he
has lifted them both and has one hand on each waist,
but the tighter his grip, the more they squirm. The
drifting lights divert his gaze—and that's when the
girls fall.

❖ ❖ ❖

Red Koko retrieves the boy, glowers at him over puffs
of smoke. "Remember, the rich are only good for
their money."

But one day when the father comes for the boy, he's
carrying shoes, pin-striped pants, a white starched shirt,
a suit coat, and a short-crowned hat. After that, it's
weekly visits to the house with the giggling twin girls.

❖ ❖ ❖

Koko makes the boy wear the suit and takes him to a
noisy hall. Sawdust and animal smells. Men in long

jackets, suits, and slouch hats in a three-story pit theater. Guffawing faces, wildly pumping fists. One man standing at the handrail keeps whipping off his stovepipe hat, orbiting it, and crying, "Beastly to lose, awfully beastly to lose!"

In the pit, dozens of rats scurry into piles in the corners, where they scramble up each others' backs. A short-haired dog grabs a rat, shakes it dead, and tosses it to the side. A man in the pit claps and points, spurring him on.

"Three minutes!" cries another man, who studies a silver pocket watch in between collecting the dead rats by their tails.

The boy grips the rail, leans forward. "None of them escape?"

Red Koko's cheeks cave as he pulls smoke through his pipe's body. "*Nyet.*"

Three men try to pull the greased head off a live gander hung by its feet. It writhes with each attempt until the head pops off with a sucking sound. A pair of cocks fight. The boy cheers when the bird he picked wins. Koko claps him on the back. Then two women, bare to the waist, climb into the pit. The men roar. The women purple each other's chest with their fists. The boy has already chosen a favorite—the tall, broad-shouldered one with small breasts—when she wrenches back the other woman's black bangs. The boy's hands freeze. Pink lines fan across the woman's face from cheek to chin: Angel.

Koko rocks back with laughter.

Then the boy's running, escaping. Koko's voice trails behind—"Where to, *kukla*?"—but he's already gone.

❖ ❖ ❖

The boy runs past the theaters and streetlamps, the tittering women in doorways, the dwellings with shuttered windows, the shanties, the barrel fires. He runs until he enters a sudden belt of darkness, where masts rise off brigs. At the river's edge, the boy strips off the jacket and trousers, the shiny shoes, and flings them into the water. He stands in his underpants, skin glistening.

At the mouth of a tunnel that empties into the river, an old woman murmurs beside a damp fire that steams and pops and sends up sour smoke. She beckons him with a wave and holds up a coat. As he nears, he sees that it's stitched together of motley scraps. The witch's mouth pinches together under a face as dry as sod. He turns his back and lets her drape the coat over his shoulders.

❖ ❖ ❖

The boy wakes to excruciating pain in his groin. He's lying inside the tunnel. In his mouth, the taste of fungus. Dried blood is caked on his thigh and his penis is too sensitive to touch. Outside the tunnel, a streak of moonlight ribbons the river's ripples. The witch sits in firelight, fondling a bloody ring of skin on the chain around her neck. She says, "You'll do your good work now."

The boy limps deeper into the tunnel.

❖ ❖ ❖

So he joins the inverted world. Spends his days in underground waterworks, the steam-choked tunnels and passages known only to rats. At nightfall the glow from between the wall cracks of river shanties catches a figure as it slips into the city. And when the grinding of train wheels saturates the air, the shadow darkens streetlamps with chucked rocks. No one sees who's breaking the glass, but they find suddenly that darkness has slipped over them like a collar. The shadow moves through crowds with the camouflage of a fish that shimmers briefly and then is gone. It follows men out of saloons, notes the panel houses to which the women lead them. It finds Angel outside a sailor's dance house on Water Street, her face sunken, bleary, her gaze sweeping from within its cage of scars.

"What do you want, ragamuffin?"

"Where's Mathilde?"

She squints. "Do you work for the almond eyes now? Have you got some smoke for us?"

The shadow even trails Red Koko, who has no time for shadows. And when the beggar children, who *can* see the boy inside the shadow, persist in pressing their wares, he knocks the tidbits out of their hands and steals their matchsticks.

❖ ❖ ❖

The men in blue flannel uniforms and sturdy leather hats hold belching hoses. The silver buttons on their jackets flicker and dance. At the curb the massive steam engine belches. The Italians were gone, the cellar overrun with sewage flowing in from the street. Rags and papers stuffed into the rafters did the trick. The shadow boy, seamed among spectators, admires the curtains of flame. They roar like a trumpet blast. Windows crumple. Bricks crack. Walls clap down.

The boy watches. He wants to find the fuse that will set the whole world on fire.

❖ ❖ ❖

Lookouts on the city's seven bell towers are doubled, patrolmen and roundsmen in the bowery trebled. They shake door handles, peer through peepholes on iron shutters, lurk in darkened doorways. Still, the panel houses and dance halls and saloons erupt in flame. The fence around the bridge is fortified and a night guard set at the construction site to stop the women from throwing themselves into the river. Instead, they make their way to the water's edge and walk into the current with bricks sewn into their dresses. Their swollen corpses are found in the following days floating on open water, tapping the side of a harbored ship, sprawled on a beachfront.

❖ ❖ ❖

Koko steps off eight paces from the sycamore and digs. His beard is singed, the sheepskin curls of his coat blackened. Soon enough, his fingertips cinch around the box. He takes out the necktie, the watch, the horn. Turns them over. Smells their rich scent.

❖ ❖ ❖

Mathilde is still at the Madam's. The boy lurks in the dark on a brownstone ledge and watches her study the items on the table: the necktie, the timepiece, the tin horn. Koko is there, gaunt and sallow, as is the father with his red scarf, and the Madam, who darkens the room and sets a candle beside a mirror. She passes a stone hung from a chain over the items. Her lips move, her eyes dance. In the glass appear the river's watery darkness, the tunnel's mouth, and a line of lights the boy has never seen.

❖ ❖ ❖

Lights. Thousands of them newly strung along the bridge, which has just opened for traffic. The lights set the river aglow and draw the boy from the tunnel. There at the mouth, unbelievably, asleep in his sheepskin coat on a bed of rocks, lies Red Koko, cradling the boy's belongings. The boy finds the heaviest rock he can lift, one as big as a market basket. He sneaks up on the giant. It takes all his might to heft the rock overhead. He wobbles under its weight. The lights hum and he lets it come down. The giant's head splits from crown to nape in a puff of straw.

A familiar voice trails out from the dark. "Thought you'd kill Red Koko tonight, did you? I'm no *kukla* like you." The giant's silhouette darkens a swath of the bridge lights. He pulls the whip from his waist. "Even a sick wolf can handle a lamb."

The boy's strength flees. He becomes as fragile as porcelain. Koko raises the whip. Then comes the tinkle of glass breaking. Tiny explosions. Sparks falling. Under it all, a muttering.

Darkness floods everything. The boy feels the city in all its submerged fragments: a brawler swears a drunken oath, a lady brings an oyster shell to her mouth, a rag picker sews another stitch, a girl leans from a window and tilts her head at the sound of the church bell tolling. The river slides, the fish twist. The witch draws close to the giant and slips her blade between his ribs. He howls as she works it deeper. She turns it in circles until his cries run liquid.

She pulls him to her and presses her mouth to his ear like a lover. She whispers, "Light a candle for the Devil."

The ground shakes with Red Koko's collapse. She cuts the rope belt and goes to work under his clothes. She stands with his member in her hand, makes some strange gestures, then underhands it into the river. Silver bodies dart to the waxy glow. Fish nibble and gorge as they follow it down. Together the old woman and the boy roll the giant's corpse into the water, where the current takes it away.

She hands the boy the necktie and timepiece. Turns to face the water and draws her nails lovingly along the tin horn. It seems for a moment that she might sound its trumpet and transform into a beautiful young woman. But she only caresses its curve and pays the boy no mind.

The spell is broken. He's no longer her slave: this he knows.

❖ ❖ ❖

"We're prepared to care for you, Cyrus, to raise you as a boy ought to be raised." The father, in his red scarf, urges him onto the elevated train.

They sit beside men drifting to sleep with ink-stained hands woven together in their laps. The train jolts, then they're moving at speed, whirling along in the dark past halos of gaslight and through great metal arches. They sweep east over a tangle of houses. Switches rattle. The boy recognizes Chatham Square, its saloons ablaze with light. He can almost hear the piano and violin music, the drunken cries, the weeping—as an instant later it's all erased by the screech of latticed pipe works.

The train rushes uptown. The city below is a dark sea. Then a yellow eye winks open in the dark: a depot's clock face. The hands look like a man slowly trying to sit up.

"I have a question," Cyrus says.

The father leans in. The train rushes on.

❖

AGONY OF THE
FORGOTTEN

Those dying here, the lonely
forgotten by the world
their tongue becomes for us
the language of an ancient planet.
CZESLAW MILOSZ, "CAMPO DEI FIORI"

For what seems like ages I've dreaded this visit to
forgotten comrades. In a deserted corner of the
country in a rundown infirmary in a quarantined,
silent chamber, I find them. With winter's blue light
seeping through the window, they keep a three-sided
deathwatch over one another. Franklin was always the
strongest, and I recognize immediately which bunk
is his. I creep forward into the blueness.

The chilly light coats Franklin's face, a gnarled
stump of skin that has spread over a grimy bandage
like a tree trunk around a garroting wire. I touch his
shoulder, and his unbandaged eye opens to reveal a
green iris rimmed in pink. The sight dizzies me. He
leans over, grunts, then bobs his head. A string of
syringes on his belt rattles as he clambers down to

shake hands. He remains silent, perhaps not wanting to undo the room's quiet. His flattened palm he presses against my chest with a softness that I understand is meant as an inquiry into my health.

"Excellent," I say with a heartiness that opens a rift between us even though Franklin's lopsided grin doesn't diminish.

He whispers, "Welcome to Golgotha. The pale priest stays the king of terrors."

"Getting along, then?" I say.

"Welcome to Gothgola. The king of terrors stays the priest pale." Franklin's pink-and-green eye bores into me.

From our time together as soldiers, certain memories remain unforgettable: choking down the slop they called rations; sneaking away from camp to bathe in the pond at the base of the waterfall; Hildegard catching a rabbit outside the perimeter and wringing its neck with his bare hands, its awful squawks we imagined reaching all the way to the commander. I expected to tell and retell these memories, but the blue air, crackling and frozen, dampens any spirit of raucous camaraderie.

I've come fresh from the outside world, where we live at a faster pace with vigor and industry, where no one thinks about these men and their suffering. I've even brought a picture from when we all belonged to that world. In it the four of us stand at the edge of a desert camp. Franklin and Hildegard stare defiantly forward, their guns pointed at the camera. Lucido kneels, his rifle aimed at the ground. I'm leaning nearly out of the picture, my elbow resting against something not in the frame. If Franklin's mind is gone, then the others will be in worse shape. Barbs of guilt sting me for not making this visit sooner.

These men are comrades. We've lain facedown in mud flavored with each other's piss; during the war we knew each others' bodies head-to-toe, could recognize an individual gait at a thousand yards; have seen each other weep. The only things that separated us were different names and identity numbers. We were an unbreakable unit. Yet here Franklin stands bobbing and shifting, his legs twisted like two warped saplings, and the veins on his bald arms and neck black rivulets. The exposed half of his face makes me want to flee its unnatural wrinkles. These three are castoffs, unredeemable men banished to a place out of the public view.

Franklin grunts and presents the walls as if unveiling a gallery of new paintings. They lean suffocatingly inward. The light at the window darkens. He clamors.

"Because you on that day said you don't even know how stretched it all was. Thought to lose my own heart." His bray—*gahf-gahf-gahf*—transforms into wheezing then into a heaving fit. He leans over his knees, each hack as sharp as a hammer against an iron wedge. Finally, he clamps a hand over his mouth and leads me to Hildegard's bunk.

It's difficult to believe the man's alive. The wool blanket isn't long enough to cover his feet, which are so pale that they're luminescent. Eyes closed. Face a white plate of meat. Arms the color of chalk peep out from under the blanket. A magnificently swollen wrist that throbs and grows larger with each slow heartbeat. A crack in the skin at the base of his hand oozes a gouty substance that spills like finely sifted flour over the blanket. Crystallized rivulets streak from the corners of his eyelids onto his pillow.

I find a chair near the door and slump into it. Franklin retires to his bunk. My gaze sweeps across the blue and gray. It settles finally on an object at my feet. A book. *Little Book of Computations.* I open it at random and read. "So that the lines may be known/ they are to be marked in the following manner: the line that is called the first means one/ the next line above it ten/ the third hundred/ and the fourth thousand/ mark this last line with a small cross./ Starting with the small cross/ for each line you must say thousand. When there are one thousand/ ten thousand/ a hundred thousand/ a thousand times a thousand/ and as many small crosses as there are, so many thousands you must always say *mýrioi.*" The words make no sense, but the texture of the pages, rough and dry, anchors me to something. I continue to read, passing over sentences, paragraphs, whole chapters with no comprehension. Eventually the room heats and grows humid as the blue light deepens. Drowsiness approaches, but the thought of falling asleep here is too frightening. I take out the photograph. In the dark my comrades' figures have solidified into silhouettes, sharp-edged shadows against a background of light-colored sand. The edges of my image are a sfumato fading into the photo's dark corner. Tiny pieces of flue drift by, descending layer by humid layer until they arrest on the damp stone floor. One of them alights on the back of my hand, and I watch it until realizing that it's actually a mosquito engorging itself. I swat it, and its blood meal dots my skin.

The third bunk is concealed in shadow. It's Lucido's, toward which Franklin motioned and said only, "Dreamless sleep quelled down chirring cricket signs. Get sound. Sure, get sound."

His bunk is in the farthest corner of the room, yet I know I must visit him before leaving. I tiptoe toward it. Atop the cot is a dark shape. Black chunks of sloughed material soil the sheets. The man appears to have no muscle or skin at all but to be held together entirely by scab. He stretches toward me a thin, terrifying arm. I flinch, step backwards, and feel betrayal burn my face. This is Lucido, the man who cocked his head at me before our first battle and said, "Find your barbarian." His confidence always grew in inverse proportion to the hopelessness of our situation. Once, when we were pinned down by enemy fire, he said, "We've got 'em right where we want 'em," as a wild grin split his face.

His arm feels like a baton of cracked earth. Bits flake off onto my palm. His eyes, bared open in lidless sockets, fail to convey any emotion. They fix on the ceiling, where a thin-lined grid of blue grout circumscribes the edges of white tiles. His mouth cracks open, and a stabbing whine spills into the room.

Screeches and hacks erupt. Franklin scampers to Lucido's side, readies a syringe from its place on his belt, and plunges the needle into the man's limp arm. The whine pitches into a frenzied shriek. A mad cicada's call echoes out from the walls. The window light brightens.

Franklin leaps from bunk to bunk like an ape. He lands on the thin windowsill, then launches into the room's upper spaces. He clutches a pipe near the ceiling, sets the light strobing as his legs sweep past the window again and again. I'm no longer aware of standing, only the rush of Franklin overhead. Now he straddles Lucido's bunk, and I'm gazing up at him as he disembowels a pillow. Its insides burst forth. Franklin flails the remnants overhead as Lucido screeches and thrashes in a prone frenzy under the shower. The atmosphere dries, becomes thinner. Breath comes easier.

Finally the sounds diminish and the motion slows. Downy white puffs litter the room, and in the corners and along the walls I notice other soggy brown feathers.

"Seventy times seven, seventy times seven, seventy times seven," Franklin mutters from his bunk, where he clutches his knees to his chest. The ritual, I sense, is a glimpse into their isolated culture, an act both sacred and remote. I belong to the outside world. I'm no longer tied to these men in this way. There's nothing I can do for them.

"Franklin, I must leave," I say.

His pink-and-green gaze follows me past Lucido's bunk. When I'm almost to the door, he leaps up, clamps my shoulder, spins me toward Lucido. "You can't do that to him. He's a man, you know. What if it were you?"

The photograph slips from my hand and spins as it falls to the floor. I don't need to look at it to know that the fourth figure has been atomized like fog dried from a beach. What emerges is what's before me: a rusty bunk, a wool blanket, and Lucido's scorched body. I want to turn around, but I fear that there's no door. In fact, I know that there's no door. Even if there were a door, there are no legs to carry me.

Into Lucido's bunk I crawl.

My eyelids flaked off long ago. My world is a scorching field of white squares hatched by thin blue lines. All day and all night I try to hold the blue grid in place. Hildegard and I are Franklin's charges, morphine fiends the both of us. Hope exists only for the next time he'll appear. Lift and press into my arm the cool release. Then the blue lines widen and net the white, ease it into retreat, and make me a man again — walking and talking among friends, checking up on old comrades, laughing and telling of good health and happy times, cupping a wisp of angel hair as it floats by, musing over wife and children and neighbors — the visitor who rolls bits of shredded gauze between thumb and forefinger, who feels the patterns of his own fingertips.

Much too soon the blue shrinks and the white advances. That's when I rush for the door, racing away from the screams, the smells, the pain. But the blazing corona always creeps over the door's edges.

Like an unyielding sun it swallows everything from the outside in until the speck that was the door disappears and I'm nailed to this bunk and all that's left is the searing.

❖

THE RUNNER

The three of us had hiked the mountain in the middle of the night to get to the cave. No one knew we were there (or so we thought at the time), but it still seemed prudent to post a lookout. So while Charlene and Dave worked inside, I leaned against the cave mouth and kept watch on a moonless world overcast with stars. It must've been 2 a.m. when I saw the runner coming.

A pinpoint of light moved up the mountain along the trail we'd hiked a few hours ago. It traveled like a satellite across the dark, only its point was below, not above. For a time I watched it and said nothing, mesmerized by its relentless advance. When it grew in size and I could see a ghosted wash of churning legs behind it, I recognized it as a runner holding a powerful flashlight. It flicked in and out as the runner passed by trees. He was moving at top speed. I estimated that we had at most four minutes before he reached the cave.

I called down to my cohorts, and they rushed out to the cave mouth. They had extinguished their headlamps and I couldn't see their features, but I could smell the damp earth clinging to their hands. Rumors of the traces of what we'd found on our first surreptitious trip to the cave were already circulating, and we'd fielded questions from several parties, some frightened, some angry, some genuinely curious.

As the runner neared, it seemed as though he (I already thought of the runner as male) was preceded by something boxy, but the distance and the dark were still too great to make it out. Dave and Charlene took deep breaths and sighed in turn. I felt exhilarated by the situation. Each second became something to treasure.

"I wonder who sent him," I said.

"Who do you think," said Charlene, meaning the outfit that owned the cave and the mountain and the path on which the runner approached. They thought of us as thieves and meddlers, though we knew better.

"What does it matter now?" said Dave. "We'll have to try and stop him."

❖ ❖ ❖

Time grew short, but we had the drop, as they say. Only briefly did I consider suggesting that we run for it, up and over the ridge to see if we couldn't make it down the mountain's other side. Or perhaps down one of the scree fields that lined the path on either side of the trail where it neared the cave. But both options I rejected, the first because none of us could match the runner's speed and the second because it was cowardly.

We decided on an ambush. Charlene ducked back into the cave to retrieve some rope while Dave took practice swings with a short-handed shovel. That left me to watch the runner's progress, and as I did so, I chewed my cheek and felt a strange affinity for the approaching figure, as if there were no paradox in both cheering on and dreading his arrival. It was clear that he was a determined and capable fellow with a strong dedication to his task.

By the time Charlene returned, the runner's light had disappeared behind a rocky outcropping. The three of us hurried down the trail and took up position behind a boulder. Then came the footsteps, *one-two, one-two, one-two,* and, thrill of thrills, the sound of the runner's breath itself, a sharp, surprisingly full nose inhalation followed by a blasted mouth exhalation: *hff-woosh, hff-woosh, hff-woosh.* Here is the sound of your death, I thought. I tried to time it right and peeked out from behind the boulder. The runner was upon us, not ten meters away.

"Dave, now!" I called, though it was already too late.

Then Charlene, hearing the futility in my voice, bumped past me and threw herself square in the runner's path. I stumbled up after her. The runner's light wasn't a flashlight after all but a flat lamp, like a train's headlight, that was strapped to his chest. It spotlighted Charlene, her mud-spattered Carhartts and frizzy red hair. What he held in front of him, like a cafeteria tray full of food, was a rectangular box of molded plastic with switches and wires and tiny bulbs. In its center hunkered a pair of waxy gray cubes, and we understood the plan: they intended to blow us to smithereens and chalk it up to an unfortunate accident.

Charlene threw her arms wide and it looked like she would tackle him, but then Dave burst out from behind the runner, having crawled around the boulder. With both hands, Dave brandished the shovel over the runner's skull. The runner turned enough so that Dave's springy black beard and crazy eyes jumped into sight. This is it, I thought. Dave will kill the man sent to kill us and we'll be done with it.

"Wait," Charlene said. Dave paused at the last instant. Then to the runner she said, "Listen. We don't want to hurt you unless we have to. Can you imagine cooperating?"

The runner drew gasps of breath but even these were controlled in a way that suggested his endurance had hardly been tested. "What did you have in mind?" His voice came out surprisingly high and nasal.

"First of all, set that down," Charlene said and motioned with open palms to the tray.

The runner bent over, supple and easy, and placed the tray on the ground.

Charlene spoke in a weary parent's voice. "Now turn to the side. You're shining that damn thing right in my eyes."

The runner did as told and only then could I see what he was wearing. Green nylon shorts split down the sides and a white tank top emblazoned with a rainbow. A small yellow cap with a tiny bill sat atop his head. He looked like he was twenty-two years old, tops. This is what death looks like, I thought with no small amount of incredulity. This is what my death looks like.

"What's your name?" Charlene demanded.

"Victor," the runner said. He was Roman-nosed and thin, his leg and arm muscles stringy and taut. He took a step down the trail, looked as if he might turn and bolt.

Dave raised the shovel and stepped closer. "Move another inch and see what happens."

Guided by Charlene, I took the rope from her and bound the runner's hands. I thought my skin would jolt with an electric charge when I touched him, but nothing. He obliged with my duties and gave no signs of fear or resistance. His skin was slick with a sheen of sweat. I cinched the last knot and he asked, "What are you going to do with me?"

"Neutralize you," Dave said.

"I wouldn't fiddle with those," Victor said when he saw Charlene squatting in front of the tray and fingering the switches.

She ignored him, lifting the tray and carrying it down the trail. She called over her shoulder, "Tie him up in the cave. I'm going to put a big rock between this thing and us."

Relief passed through me. We had vanquished the threat.

❖ ❖ ❖

Back inside the cave, Dave and I cinched Victor's ankles together, then laid him on his side and lashed the whole caboodle of his bound body around a rock the size of a small refrigerator. Dave wanted to knock him unconscious, but I suggested that that was over-kill, not to mention criminal.

"What does it matter, now that we're in so deep?" he said but dropped his uplifted palms and headed into the cave.

Charlene returned and we started digging like mad. The three of us toiled away. The traces grew stronger and stronger. The possibilities so enchanted us and we lost ourselves in such a reverie of work that we failed to notice that the sky had lightened until Victor called from above. "I'm sorry, but if I don't do this, I'm in big trouble."

He stood at the cave mouth silhouetted by the dawn sky. The bindings lay at his feet, and then we saw that the tray did, too. A tiny blue light flashed on it. Here, I thought, fate has caught up to us after all. As much as I hated the inevitability of death, I under-stood that events would run their necessary course.

Charlene dusted off her pants and rubbed cave dirt from her palms. "And what about us?" she said. "Aren't our lives worth a hill of beans?"

"Sure they are," Victor said.

"And the discovery," Dave added. "Are you ready to write it off, too?"

"I don't know anything about that." Victor's akimbo arms carved a pair of triangles out of the sky, and those triangles grew lighter as we watched. Victor seemed to be politely waiting for something. Our last words, I thought. He wants a performance.

A compulsion rose inside me, and I winced as my teeth started in again on my cheek. That exhilaration returned from earlier in the night, when I'd first glimpsed the runner.

"You're right, Victor," I said. The unexpected strength in my voice surprised me. "If you don't do this, you'll be in trouble. They might even kill you."

Charlene and Dave spun their headlamps toward me. I held up a hand to their objections. Charlene had reasoned and defused. Dave had used force, was even then calculating the thirty seconds it would take to reach Victor. Now I would have to outwit him. I had taken his measure and saw my chance. "We're nothing to you and why should we be anything? You've got so much going for you. You're obviously a fast runner, faster than any of us. No, don't be modest. Speed, diligence, persistence, these are your strengths."

Victor stood there mute, trying to grasp where I was headed.

"But they're also a weakness. They give you a false sense of control. I understand that you have to do what you have to do, but let me ask you this. What would it look like if you decided to indulge me in my final moments and considered a request?"

"Nah," Victor said. "I'll be honest. I haven't got any backbone. I can't stand up for anything. They tell me what to do and I do it. I'm like rubber to them. They just use me—"

"—for their own purposes, yes," I said. Then it came to me, the line that would buy us passage. "We don't get to pick the life we're born into, Victor, but we do, from time to time, get to make a choice. Here, now, you can still choose." A chill of pure feeling raced through me. I could tell that my words were sinking in.

Victor rubbed his jaw. Bent to retrieve his little yellow cap and pulled it on. Then he said, "Yeah. No. I'm sorry, no choice," and hovered his foot over the tray and flipped a switch with the toe of his shoe. The blue light snapped off and a red one started flashing in its place. "I hate to do this to you and all, but you've got twenty seconds to say goodbye. There's no kill switch." Victor raised his hand in a goodbye wave, and the last we heard of him was that patterned rhythm of foot strikes, *one-two, one-two, one-two,* making their way down the trail and slipping through our senses like the final knot on a rescue rope.

Twenty seconds: an eternity! That third of a minute grew like a gift in our minds and divided and divided again until it contained whole epochs—ages! I tell you—in which to grow old and congratulate each other on accomplishments and share in the sorrow of losses and curse fate and yet persist and rise and fall—and we did, we did, only to find that a mere fraction of our allotted time had passed, and so we lived again, passing still more authentic lives back and forth in glances as we founded new personalities along new principles that granted us new fortunes that we then also outgrew. When these lives, too, had faded, we simply took stock of where we stood in that glorious cave world with the smells of damp earth and rock in the air and a mayfly drifting in.

And when we returned to our senses, we knew that never again would we feel such joy. Authentic life would forever after remain beyond our grasp. Whether it was merely a ploy to scare us off, we never did discover, but the explosives failed to detonate. We packed up our gear and hiked out, the momentous find abandoned, and in the years to come, as the memory of that morning and the sight of each other only evoked an increasingly painful sense of loss, we, Charlene, Dave, and I, grew apart.

❖

LONELY OLD WOMAN
EXTRACTS HER HEART

In my fifties I experienced something that I don't think was related to menopause. It only happened late at night after I had swaddled myself in bedcovers and blankets and shut out the world. It would start as a hypersensitivity in my chest, the nerves on high alert, until each heartbeat struck like a detonation. Only my heart wasn't racing; it was beating at its normal pace. All the same, there it was, repeatedly exploding behind my ribs.

I would find that my right hand was already inside my nightgown, resting against the skin on my chest. I know it sounds strange, but I couldn't tell where my hand ended and my chest began. More than that, I had the odd desire not to think of the two as separate. I want to be as clear as possible because I want you to know how it felt as it was happening.

It was an opening and an entering. It was also something that had already taken place; that is to say, when the conditions were right—when it was dark and quiet and warm and I felt completely safe and alone—it wasn't so much an action that occurred but a realization of something that had already transpired.

What happened was this: I would find that my heart was in my hand, heavy and alive, my actual heart. Its surface was slick and surprisingly dry. It felt like a creature that I had somehow caught in my grip. A hairless baby rabbit, maybe. Yet it had none of a rabbit's fragility. It was a working muscle, and it pulsed with a mindless insistence. It was the sensation of that jolt, so sudden and sure, coming again and again, *oosh, oosh, oosh,* expanding against my palm, that sent a cold shiver up over my scalp.

I would lie there for a long time, both believing and disbelieving what was happening. Nested away in my bed in the basement, surrounded by earth and black sky, with no one in the whole world thinking of me except perhaps you, I held my heart. I knew no one would believe me if I told them, and so I never did. No one, that is, except for you right now.

What thoughts came to me on those nights.

I thought of my mother, of how for years she worked as a floor nurse while the discs in her spine wore down, of the stories my father used to tell, and of that line on his tombstone that always appears when I try to recall his face—*Gone but not forgotten.* And I thought of you, of that moment on the verandah when you asked to see my ring and I let you hold my hand for longer than I should have.

This only happened four or five times and all in my early fifties, as I mentioned. Now I'm an old woman, but I would love nothing more than to realize, once again, that my hand had slipped inside my chest. After all, what belongs to us more than our own hearts?

SUNSHOT BOOK AWARD

FICTION · 2017

Bloodshot Stories

2017

JEFF P. JONES

FIRST PLACE ♦ SHORT STORY COLLECTION

ABOUT THE AUTHOR

JEFF P. JONES was born in Denver, and is a graduate of the University of Colorado at Denver, the University of Washington, and the University of Idaho. He lives on the Palouse in northern Idaho. He's a MacDowell Fellow, a Bread Loaf Fellow in Fiction (2018), and his writing has won a Pushcart Prize, as well as the Hackney, Meridian Editors', A. David Schwartz, Wabash, and Lamar York prizes.

His debut novel, *Love Give Us One Death*, won the George Garrett Fiction Prize in 2016, and his handbook, *Writing for the Reader: Practice in Prose Craft*, is now available on Kindle and as a paperback. *Bloodshot Stories* is his first published story collection.

JEFFPJONES.COM

ALSO BY THE AUTHOR

Writing for the Reader: Practice in Prose Craft
TROIKA PRESS, 2018

Love Give Us One Death: Bonnie and Clyde in the Last Days
TEXAS REVIEW PRESS, 2016

PUBLICATION ACKNOWLEDGMENTS

Some of these stories appeared in slightly different versions in the following journals:

Dogwood
Mississippi Review
Night Train
Post Road
Quiddity
Rambunctious Review

Redivider
Sycamore Review
The Turnip Truck(s)
Water~Stone Review
Zahir Tales

THE FUTURE IS UP FOR GRABS,
CONCEIVED BY THE IMAGINATION,
CONSTRUCTED WITH WORDS, AND
EXPLAINED AS A STORY.

SUNSHOT 𝓢 PRESS

Shot In The Head

by Lee Varon

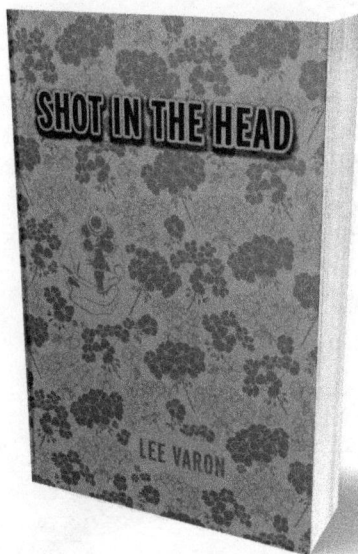

Lee Varon's poems take us to the shooting of her grandfather in 1936. The images like "a blush that turned to blood," are breath-taking. At first it is a family story, but as you examine it further, the views of prejudice in the community are jaw-dropping, yet amazingly relevant to today's issues. Her grandmother, Virginia Marie, navigates life with pride and loyalty, yet fear and bigotry, highlighting the complexity of human nature.

—Jean Flanagan

Author of *Black Lightning*

SUNSHOT PRESS

2017 SUNSHOT BOOK PRIZE™ FOR NONFICTION

Human Rights and Wrongs

Reluctant Heroes Fight Tyranny

by Adrianne Aron

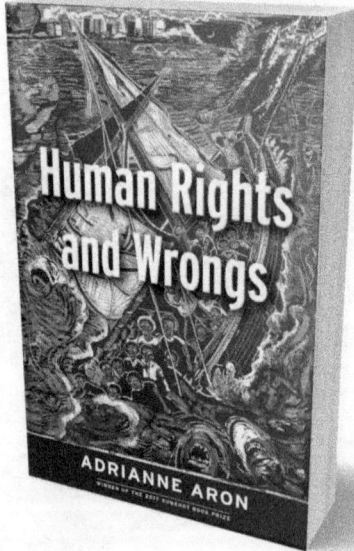

A clever joker once said, 'I dream of a world where chickens can cross the road without having their motives questioned.' I, as a mental health professional, dream of one where psychologists will understand why Ernesto Cruz drinks himself into a stupor, why Eva refuses to speak about what happened to her in Honduras, why Mrs. Malek is afraid to return to Afghanistan. In a collection of serious yet entertaining human interest stories, Adrianne Aron's Human Rights and Wrongs *engages the general reader while inspiring psychologists to think outside the box.*

— Shawn Corne, Ph.D.

Clinical Psychologist, Albany, California

SUNSHOT PRESS

2017 SUNSHOT BOOK PRIZE™ FOR FICTION

An Incomplete List of My Wishes

by Jendi Reiter

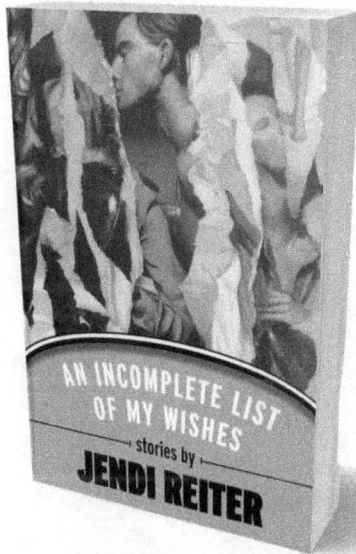

Jendi Reiter is a masterful short story writer. Truth and humor are woven intricately, ripe with emotion and stripped down to the bone. You will read these again and again.

—Jacqueline Sheehan

New York Times bestselling author of *Lost and Found* (William Morrow) and *The Tiger in the House* (Kensington)

SUNSHOT PRESS

SUNSHOT PRESS WOULD NOT HAVE BEEN POSSIBLE WITHOUT THE BOLD SUPPORT OF THE FOLLOWING POETS & WRITERS:

Barbara A.   Adrianne A.   T. A.   David A.   Idris A.   Kaye A.   Thomas J.   Paul M

Samantha T.   Linda F.   Craig O.   Gary P.   LeeAnn P.   Brian P.   Gary P.   T. M.

Ron V.   Marina H.   Eric W.   Sandra W.   Stuart W.   Emma W.   Fred W.

Rebecca L.   Barbara D.   Dana C.   Elaine C.   Kristen C.   Patricia B.

Timothy W.   James W.   Cynthia W.   Fred W.   Jeanne W.   Lee V.

Benjamin B.   Claire B.   Jerome   Marge B.   Patricia B.   Ruth M.

Barbara S.   Rachel B.   Ellen A.   Patricia R.   Nancy R.   Vincent J.

Alfred M.   Gregory S.   Jan S.   Catherine S.   James S.   Harvey S.

Lisa P.   Luke W.   Leland J.   Gail W.   Lillo W.   Pam W.   Lyzette W.

Terri M.   Sean M.   Deana N.   Jed M.   Barbra N.   Joel N.   Paul N.

Mara S.   Ramon B.   Bruce R.   John R.   Jendi R.   Paddy R.   Susan P.

Stanley R.   Andrew S.   Lynn S.   Kathryn P.   Anneliese S.   Mick S.

Lones S.   Corey M.   Richard S.   Nathan S.   Andrew S.   Elaine S.

J.D. B.   Roberta D.   Susan S.   Victoria S.   Joanne S.   Jen S.

Felix N.   Evelyn V.   Derek U.   Mike T.   Naomi M.   Jayshiro T.

Simone M.   Aida Z.   Cindy Z.   Paula Z.   Allan Y.   Felice W.

Tori M.   Karen H.   Ken M.   Barbara M.   Matt M.   Sean M.

Anca H.   David H.   Dennis H.   Eileen H.   Linda H.   W. H.

Kate H.   Jack H.   Roberta H.   Eunice H.   Nancy H.

Jonathan G.   Bruce G.   Joshua B.   Thomas B.   Catherine B.   Enid H.

Susan C.   Danny C.   Laurie C.   Julius C.   Richard B.   R.C. G.   Adam G.

Casey C.   Garry C.   LaRue C.   Bob R.   Kathy C.   Susan C.   Margo B.

Rusty D.   Effie D.   Deborah D.   Annie D.   Howard G.

Bill G.   Tina G.   Nina G.   Paula F.   Jon F.

Jerri B.   Kathryn C.   Robynn C.   Greer G.

William E.   Mary D.   Frank D.   George D.

Ruth F.   Benjamin F.   Teressa E.   Renato E.

Chad F.   Andrew H.   Ann H.   Lorien H.   Jeff J.   Martin I.   Mark H.

Christina F.   Ellen L.   John L.   David L.   Djelloul M.   Bernard M.

Richard L.   Jeffrey M.   Kevin M.   Peter M.   Wendell M.   Clif M.

Genese G.   Howard E.   Alison L.   Kurt L.   Naomi L.   Sam L.

Albert L.   Patricia B.   Chad B.   Mark B.   David B.   Julia L.

Roberta G.   Olaf K.   Kristie L.   Jacqueline L.   Lee L.   Thom K.

Joanne G.   Francis J.   Joyce K.   Marylou S.   Peter K.

James C.   Jason H.   Ryan H.   Georganne H.   Cleda H.

Joan C.   Edie C.

Leslee B.

Beth C.

Jackie M.

THANK YOU

SUNSHOTS.ORG

SUNSHOT ⓢ PRESS

CPSIA information can be obtained
at www.ICGtesting.com
Printed in the USA
FSHW010242240819
61386FS